A Novel for Young Adults

The
ROAD
to the
VALLEY

by VIRGINIA NIELSEN

Illustrated by Vana Earle

DAVID McKAY COMPANY, Inc.   NEW YORK

DEDICATION

This book is for my nieces and nephews,
all thirty-four of them—and for Robin,
who wanted me to write *her* a book.

THE ROAD
TO THE VALLEY

"Salt Lake City,
Oct. 18, 1849

... I heard last night that an express had come in from the Mormon camp, near the South Pass, and that the snow around their wagons was four feet deep. I fear some of the poor creatures will have cold feet before they get through. ..."

—Letters by Forty-niners,
Edited by DALE L. MORGAN

Prologue

O NE of the great stories of the Bible is Exodus, the story of Moses leading the Israelites from Egypt into the Promised Land. Our own shores were settled by the Pilgrims, who came to the New World seeking the freedom to worship God in their own way. Two centuries later, a great modern exodus played a part in the settling of our west when a people dubbed "Mormon" by their enemies followed their leader, Brigham Young, into the wilderness, seeking freedom from religious persecution.

The Mormons were members of a new church organized in New York state in 1830 by a young man named Joseph Smith. He claimed to be a prophet who had talked with God and to have translated the Book of Mormon from ancient plates of gold given him by an angel. This was regarded as effrontery by some people, and for seventeen years the converts to the new church were mocked, beaten—sometimes murdered—and driven out of their burning homes in settlement after settlement.

In 1844 Joseph Smith and his brother, Hyrum, were

jailed in Carthage, Illinois, then shot in their jail cell by an angry mob. Two stormy years later, the Mormons were once again driven from their homes in the beautiful city of Nauvoo which they had built on the banks of the Mississippi River in Illinois. This time the decision was made to leave the United States and seek a refuge beyond the Rocky Mountains.

Their new leader, Brigham Young, wrote to James K. Polk, President of the United States: *"We will go so far that our enemies will not choose to follow us, and we will pick so unpromising a place that nobody will covet it."*

At that time the Missouri River was the border between Iowa Territory, soon to become a state, and Indian country. The Omahas felt kindly toward these white men who also had been pushed farther and farther west. After concluding a treaty of friendship with their chief, Big Elk, the Mormon leader established his people in winter camps on both sides of the river. When spring came, he led a small pioneer party on a journey of exploration across the plains and over the Rockies into the valley of the Great Salt Lake. *"This is the place,"* he told his followers.

But a whole people moves slowly. It moves from camp to camp and some are left behind for several years until they can earn money for the journey. In 1846 the United States declared war on Mexico, and many of the Mormon men who enlisted left their families on the Missouri frontier, still yearning for the "promised land."

CHAPTER 1

Ellen Barlow held her gray linsey skirt near her shoetops as she picked her way through the mudholes left by the rapidly melting snow.

Like a trembling in the air, like a vibration from the earth under her feet, she could feel the stir of excitement that was quickening the settlement on the banks of the Missouri now that April was here, and her own pulse quickened in tune.

In a few weeks the wagons would begin crossing the river that marked the Iowa frontier and assembling beyond the other shore, in Omaha country. Then the first wagon train of the season would crawl out like a giant white caterpillar on the prairie road that stretched almost endlessly toward the place her mother always referred to in one breath as "Zion-where-the-Saints-are-gathering—" the valley of the Great Salt Lake.

"And this time we'll be with them," Ellen thought,

1

yearningly—she and Joey and Mama and Papa. For surely Papa would be returning for them now that the snows were melting!

She repressed an impulse to skip—after all, she was almost sixteen years old!—but her feet twinkled beneath the long full skirt, and a golden eagerness danced in her eyes.

The path she was following wound downward from the heights called by the Indians the Council Bluffs, and she could look across the cluster of graying, peeled-log buildings and the wide stretch of the river to a flatboat tied up on the opposite shore. A group of bearded horsemen were approaching it and she inspected them with lively curiosity.

Below her, faint shadows of green showed on dirt roofs as the seeds of last year's grasses sprouted. Brighter in the sun was the white of new canvas on the wagons that dotted the townsite. As the snow melted, Ellen fancied the town was turning white again with canvas. Every day there were more wagons, every day tents mushroomed at the edges of the settlement.

Last week a steamer from New Orleans had deposited its load of pale and weary passengers from far-off England to swell the tent city on the shore. Since then the wagon shops and the tin shops had filled the day and night with the noise of their furious activities—saws whining, hammers pounding, anvils ringing—as they tried to fill the orders for fit-outs for the newcomers.

Ellen looked again at the travel-stained horsemen

and their pack animals gathering on the western shore. They must have come a long way, all the way from the Great Salt Lake, perhaps, through the snowy passes of the Rockies, bringing letters from Brigham Young and the Saints who were already gathered with him. They might even have come from the fabulous new gold fields of California.

Her heart skidded as she thought, "They could be soldiers of the Battalion. One of them could be Papa!" She resolved to meet the flatboat. There would be just time to go to the store first.

In a few moments she had reached the level of the settlement at the water's edge. The sun was stronger down here, and the air that touched her face felt damp and had a warm, brackish odor. She pushed her bonnet back from the damp tendrils of hair on her forehead and directed her steps more slowly toward the chinked log building that bore a sign lettered, "D. B. Atkins, Genl. Mdse."

The interior of the store was cool and dark and redolent with fragrances from the smoked meats hanging from the rafters, the open barrels of dried fruits, and the calico dyestuffs on the shelves. Another acrid odor, unmistakably Indian, came from the tanned buckskin clothing worn by three Pottawattamie Indians standing silent and impassive around the empty stove.

A little apart from them were two men she knew and saw frequently at church. The taller of the two, a man with piercing black eyes in a bearded face, smiled at her.

"Hello, Ellen. How is your mother?"

"Fine, thank you, Brother Safford." The expression came naturally to her lips. All Mormons were "brother" and "sister" to each other.

"Diantha—Zina." His two daughters turned from the counter. Behind them Brother Atkins, his smooth-shaven face as sour as if he had bit into a green apple, was measuring a length of "factory," as everyone called the cheap, unbleached cotton goods that had so many uses on the frontier.

"You know Ellen Barlow," Brother Safford said.

"Oh, hello, Ellen," Diantha said carelessly, and her sister murmured, "Hello."

Ellen greeted them with reserve. She resented the fact that Brother Safford had had to remind his daughters to speak. They were a year or two older than she and she thought them very pretty, but rather stuck-up. They both had their father's sparkling dark eyes but Diantha's skin was like fine porcelain while Zina had the dark olive look of a gypsy and sometimes, Ellen had heard, stained her lips with the juice from red berries.

They both looked beyond Ellen at someone who had entered the store behind her. She turned her head and saw a tall young man with hair as yellow as ripe corn and eyes that looked at her with a teasing brightness, almost as if he knew her! Ellen was sure she had never seen him before, and she turned her gaze away in some confusion, wondering if he came from the tent city of the immigrants.

Brother Atkins was taking down a bolt of sprigged muslin and Ellen thought with a fleeting longing that it would make a lovely Sunday dress. It seemed out of place in this rough store with its overpowering smells, bringing back a gracious world Ellen had almost forgotten, of comfortable brick houses with white fences around them, and stores whose shelves held bolts of silk stuffs and boxes of feathers and flowers and other feminine treasures.

"Please, Papa? Please?" Diantha and Zina were begging for lengths of the sprigged muslin, but Brother Safford said, "It won't be very practical on the plains." He explained to the man standing with him, "I am getting ready to leave with the first company this spring."

"Papa, we won't be able to buy anything so pretty in the Valley. Oh, please!"

"We'll see."

As the two girls fingered the stuff and chattered about patterns, Ellen felt envy crowd her heart. Her gray linsey was over two years old and much too warm for summer.

Another woman had entered the store and stood beside Ellen, waiting. Brother Atkins laid the muslin to one side and looked past Ellen. "Sister Alice, how are you today?"

"He knows I came in first," Ellen thought. But she

waited quietly while Sister Alice took her time deciding on a pattern of calico.

When she left the old storekeeper said to one of several men who had entered, "What can I do for you, Brother?"

The man gestured toward Ellen. "This young lady has been waiting—"

"I'll get to you in a moment, Ellen." Brother Atkins' tone was impatient and somewhat familiar.

Ellen nodded, flushing, conscious of the eyes of the yellow-haired stranger at the end of the counter.

The old storekeeper began to grumble, in a low voice as though to indicate it were a private conversation, but loud enough so all could hear. "Something must be done about these destitute families of the soldiers. For two years and more I have carried some of them on my books."

The man to whom he spoke sent an apologetic glance toward Ellen. "Brother Brigham promised the men who enlisted in the Battalion that their families would be cared for."

"Brother Brigham promised and we have to pay," the storekeeper said sourly. "He took all the Saints who had goods and possessions on with him to Zion. We who stayed behind with the poor must support them."

"But we all support them, Brother Atkins," a cheerful voice cut in. "To hear you talk a body would think you were the only one who gave his tenth day's labor to the poor."

"A tenth day's labor!" The old man's voice rose testily. "My books are full of accounts of soldiers' families I never expect to collect. A business cannot be run that way, Brigham Young or no Brigham Young!"

From somewhere near the door a new voice said loudly, "I marched with the Mormon Battalion, Brother Atkins, two thousand miles afoot through the mountains to Santa Fé and across the desert to San Diego! Would you trade places with me?"

"The Mexicans are defeated and you are home, Brother," the storekeeper said drily. "But how can I collect from those who enlisted again instead of coming back to their obligations? Or those who stayed in California to work on John Sutter's mill where they claim to have found gold, while their families remain here in poverty?"

Ellen wondered if it were obvious to all that Brother Atkins was speaking especially for her. The Safford girls knew. She could hear them whispering together.

She lifted her chin. "You will sing a different song when they come back with their pockets full of gold dust," she said, with spirit, and there was approving laughter around her.

Brother Atkins did not laugh. "That is a song I would like to sing! All right, Ellen, what is it this time?"

Her cheeks still aflame, Ellen presented her small list of necessities. "A pound of sugar, some thread, and a packet of English needles."

"I have only a small stock of needles," the old storekeeper said grumpily, "and I have many customers who will want to be taking some west with them this spring."

Ellen's head lifted higher. "And so will we!"

Behind her Brother Safford said in a voice of stern authority, "Brother Atkins, I will personally guarantee Sister Barlow's account. Please give Ellen whatever she needs."

Ellen turned her flushed face. "Thank you, Brother Safford, but my father will be coming home now that the snows are melting." She waited only until she could pick up her purchases, then turned blindly toward the square of sunlight that was the open door.

She had to pass the tall young man with the yellow hair and she turned her head sharply so she would not have to see the expression in his eyes. She could not bear to find either sympathy or pity there.

But as she passed him she felt something pushed into her hand. She looked up in astonishment.

His eyes were dancing with mischief and he had his finger to his lips. Ellen drew a sharp quick breath. Then, having barely hesitated, she walked sedately out of the store.

She was trembling all over with emotions she could no longer repress. She hurried around the corner of the building and there opened her hand and looked down at a *dried peach half!* Laughter bubbled to her lips, but the sting of tears was in her eyes.

Someone was coming toward her and she quickly slipped the dried fruit into her pocket and turned toward the river. If only her father were on that flatboat!

CHAPTER 2

The yearning to go to the valley of the mountains that Ellen Barlow and her mother shared with nearly every other family in the encampment on the Missouri River was the hunger of a homeless people for a place of their own.

Her mother and father belonged to the new religious group known as the Church of Jesus Christ of Latter-day Saints, but called by their neighbors Mormons, in mocking reference to the ancient book which the Angel Moroni had given to their prophet, Joseph Smith, on plates of hammered gold.

All her life Ellen had heard stories about how the Saints, as they called themselves, had been driven from their Missouri homes, often in the middle of the night, by cursing, bullying, haystack-burning mobs. She had been old enough to remember the grief and consternation with which her people had heard the

9

news of the prophet's death at the hands of his enemies in 1844. And only three years ago she herself had experienced the violence of a mob in Illinois.

She shivered, remembering that nightmare winter of '46 when armed men had run through the streets of the Mormon city of Nauvoo setting fire to houses and stores, firing on the Saints who tried vainly to protect their property and the temple they had so painstakingly built.

That was when her embittered and disillusioned people had resolved to find a place of their own beyond the Rocky Mountains. In the snow and ice of February, carrying with them only what they could put into their wagons, the Barlows and other families of Nauvoo had traveled across the prairies and swamps of Iowa Territory.

Before they reached the Missouri, twelve thousand homeless people living in great camps they called "camps of Israel," the United States had declared war with Mexico and Brigham Young, the Saints' new leader, had been asked to furnish a battalion of soldiers to fight for California.

Five hundred Mormons volunteered. Ellen's father had marched away with them, leaving his family in a home that was little more than a cave he had hastily dug in the bluff above the Missouri River.

When spring came, Brigham Young had taken a hundred and forty-three men and made an exploration trip across the plains to the Rocky Mountains to select the site of the new city the Saints would build on the shores of the Great Salt Lake, and to build homes and plant crops which the Saints coming after them could harvest.

Last summer, the summer of '48, Ellen and her mother and Joey had said good-by to hundreds of friends and watched a stream of new converts to the church set out across the plains to join the Saints in Zion, while they waited impatiently behind for Thaddeus Barlow to return for them.

Oh, he must be on his way home to them!

Picking her way through the mudholes and between some ox-drawn wagons and horse-drawn buggies waiting to cross on the flatboat, Ellen joined a group of people gathered near the bank. Wide and deceptively swift, the river was swollen now with melted snow and spring rains. It glittered like fragments of a mirror, each reflecting the low sun into her face.

"Hello, Ellen. Are you expecting your father?"

She turned toward the woman who had spoken, recognizing a friend of her mother's. Her face was transfigured.

"My husband is on the boat," she said, with quiet joy, and Ellen's heart leaped. The woman's husband had marched away with Ellen's father.

"I heard last night from a brother who met their party while he was out hunting. I'm sorry I didn't think to let you know, Ellen, but he didn't mention your papa."

It was strange no one had come to tell them. "It's all right." Ellen moved nearer, standing in full view of the approaching boat. Could one of those strange bearded men be Thad Barlow? If she did not know him he would surely know her.

A familiar shout came to her ears. She turned her head quickly and saw her young brother running between two canvas tents nearby with another boy close behind him.

She shrieked, "Joey!" but he had disappeared. What was he doing down here among the tents of the English immigrants?

While she looked uneasily after him the flatboat was tying up just below, and presently the weary, dirty travelers were leading their animals up the steep cut to the bank.

Ellen saw her mother's friend go flying, her calico skirts swirling out behind her and her woollen shawl slipping from her shoulders. A great red-bearded man caught her up in his arms and Ellen turned her gaze sharply away to search the next face appearing above the bank, and the next.

At last one man who had glanced into her eager eyes and looked away, turned back. "Aren't you Thad Barlow's daughter?"

She nodded, struck dumb by something frightening in his face.

"Is your mother in good health?"

The man just behind him said, "He means can Sister Barlow stand a shock?"

Fear grew in Ellen's breast until it pressed against her heart. She blinked her eyes, wishing a childish wish that their sober, hollow-cheeked faces would disappear.

"It's Ellen, isn't it?" the first man said gently. And when she nodded, "Will you take us to your mother, Ellen?"

She led them up the zigzagging path she had descended earlier. The sun dipped lower across the river, casting squat shadows against the hillside as they climbed. Ellen pointed out the dugout that was her home.

It was a curious dwelling, half cave and half cabin, but Ellen had grown used to it now. She pushed open the heavy door, calling, "Mama, I've company with me."

There was only one room, hollowed out of the hillside, its rear walls and sloping floor of earth, roofed and fronted with chinked logs over which lengths of factory muslin had been nailed. Beds pegged into the walls on each side of the door and covered with buffalo robes served as seats by day. Looking somewhat out of place were a handsome small cherry chest and a rocker near the hearth.

Her mother's face was a white blur as she turned from the fireplace at the rear of the dugout where she was cooking something in a three-legged spider nestled in the hot coals.

She came toward them, saying, "It's Brother Tom Brewer, isn't it? Is it really you? But how weary you look!"

Sudden high color had dyed her cheeks. Ellen

thought how handsome her mother was, with her great dark eyes and her high-piled dark hair.

The tall man who had recognized Ellen said, "Sister Harriet, this is Brother Angell. We've just come from the Salt Lake Valley, and it's been a hard trip with the snow not yet gone from the mountains."

"And you've come straight here! You've brought news of Thad?"

"Bad news, I'm afraid, ma'am," Brother Angell said in a soft southern voice.

Ellen saw her mother falter and moved swiftly to her side.

"He's not coming home?" her mother guessed. She sank abruptly to the edge of the nearest bunk. "What—happened?"

"Indians," Tom Brewer said. "At least, it was done with arrows and tomahawk—" His companion gave him a look and he went on hastily, "It happened when we left California late last summer. They were a day's journey ahead of us in the mountains, scouting. We found their camp the morning after it happened."

"There were others?" Ellen's mother asked faintly.

"Thad and two others who had stayed behind like us to work a year in the gold fields."

"Last summer," her mother repeated, and Ellen knew what she was thinking: *Last summer—and all this time they hadn't known.*

Brother Brewer was explaining, "We reached the Salt Lake Valley in November and had to winter there."

"They were carrying their savings in gold dust," Brother Angell put in.

"Gold dust!" Harriet Barlow said bitterly. "If he'd come back without it, we'd be in Zion now with the Saints!"

"He wanted it for your trip across the plains, Sister Harriet."

"We'd be in Zion," she repeated, and buried her face in her hands.

CHAPTER 3

ELLEN wished her mother could weep. Tears would be better than this frozen silence as Harriet Barlow moved from the fireplace to the rude table preparing their supper as usual.

She was relieved when her mother asked, "Where is Joey?"

Ellen opened her mouth to say she had seen him down among the tents on the river's edge, then thought better of it. "He is probably bringing Daisy-Very-Gently in."

The image of her father was all at once very vivid, as she remembered the day her mother had named the little cow, laughing at her father's efforts to milk her at her first freshening.

"Gently, now, Daisy," he kept saying. "Gently, gently." And as the frisky cow edged away and rolled a suspicious eye at him, he entreated, "Very gently,

16

Daisy!" causing her mother to go off into peals of laughter that frightened Daisy into kicking up her heels again.

They had brought Daisy-Very-Gently with them from Nauvoo when the mob came and there was time to load, and room to bring only their few choicest possessions.

Daisy's milk had been their chief food these difficult years since Thad Barlow marched away with the Battalion. Now that the grasses were coming up where the snow had melted, Daisy was staked out to browse on the hillside, and it was ten-year-old Joey's duty to herd her. If he did not bring her in soon, he would be milking by lantern again.

"I'll just go and see if I can see them coming," Ellen said. With so many strangers in the settlement fitting out for the plains, a pretty little cow like Daisy might be a temptation. "Will you be all right, Mama?"

Her mother did not answer. Deeply troubled, Ellen stepped outside and climbed a slanting pathway to another dugout.

The sun was almost down and the river shone like a bronze serpent beyond the roofs of the settlement. The air was delicate and still; early evening sounds lay softly on it. She heard the tinkle of bells and the lowing of cattle as other animals were being brought in for milking, but Daisy's bell, a sound that had an exquisite familiarity for her, was missing.

Small red-headed children tumbled out of the open door of the neighboring dugout and Ellen greeted them absently, her brows drawn together with responsibility.

"Hello, Ellen," said a plump young woman, coming to the doorway with a red-haired baby in her arms. She had a wide friendly smile and a face covered with freckles, and her hair was the same bright shade as her baby's.

"Sister Sarah, could you go and sit with Mama for a while? I'm worried to leave her alone."

"What's the matter?" the woman asked in quick sympathy. When she heard Ellen's story, she gave a brisk set of orders. To a tall boy with pale red hair curling over his ears she said, "You go down to the river and look for Joey. Stop on the way and tell Sister Andrews she's needed at Sister Barlow's. Emma Andrews will be good for your mama," she explained to Ellen.

To a girl about eight years old whose hair curled in bright ringlets she said, "You watch the stew and mind you don't let it burn. If I'm not home by dark, go ahead and feed the young'uns and put them in bed. I'll just take the baby along with me. Now don't you worry about a thing, Ellen. You run along and find your Daisy. She's too good a cow to lose."

Ellen thanked her and took the path that zigzagged down the bluff. The cow must have pulled her stake and wandered to the bottoms lying south of the settlement.

The sun had disappeared beyond the river, leaving a smoky orange afterglow. Lights twinkled in the settlement as lamps were lit, mere pinpricks of brightness in the mist that was creeping up from the river.

As she walked, Ellen called, stopping now and then to listen for Daisy's bell. When she reached the bottom, the ground was springy underfoot. Ahead, tall cottonwoods made dark clumps marking the bend of the river which gleamed dully, seeming to have imprisoned some of the vanished light.

The marsh lay silently in wait for her, not making itself known until her foot sank in treacherous mud, then making a noisy sucking sound as she pulled out. There was a monotonous chorus of small shrill frogs, the occasional chitter of a sleepy bird, and the buzz of pesky mosquitoes she kept slapping away. Once she heard a man's laugh, distant but carrying clearly across the marsh.

After what seemed a long time a faint musical "Chink!" sounded ahead of her. She froze to attention. In a moment it was repeated.

She called, "Sook, Daisy! Sook, Daisy!" and was rewarded by a faint, familiar lowing. She plunged toward it excitedly. Soon she saw the glare from a campfire in the cottonwoods along the river.

Silhouettes moved between her and the light, and the tantalizing smell of frying beef brought a sharp pang of hunger to remind her of her empty stomach.

She came closer and what she had thought was the sizzle of meat frying in its own grease became another familiar sound. It was unmistakably the metallic sing of a sharp stream of milk hitting the side of a bucket.

Breathless and muddy, she hurried into the circle of light. A bearded man looked up from the skillet laid across rocks in the fire and got to his feet. But Ellen was looking beyond him. A few feet away a second man had Daisy tied with her rope to a wheel of their wagon and was down on his knees milking her!

"That's my cow!" Ellen exclaimed.

The man milking turned his head against Daisy's flank. He winked at the standing man, who was grinning so that his white teeth showed through his dark beard.

"What makes you think she's your cow?"

Ellen called, "Sook, Daisy! Sook, Daisy!"

Daisy rolled her eyes and took a step. The milker snatched up his bucket just in time to save it from being overturned, almost falling backward in his awkward haste.

His companion burst into rude laughter. Ellen flew to Daisy and began untying her. But the man nearest set down his pail of milk and grabbed Daisy's collar, making her bell ring sharply.

"Now you wait a minute, girlie! This here little cow's a stray."

"She's not a stray!" Ellen said, angrily. "She's belled, and she answers to her name. She's our cow!" Her face felt flushed, and the strings of her sunbonnet overtight.

The man's weasel face changed. "She's a pretty little thing, ain't she?" he asked his companion, and Ellen knew he was not talking about the cow.

The bearded man spat expertly into the flames alongside his skillet. "Probably already married to one o' them ugly Mormons with a harem. They marries 'em off young."

"Be you Miss or Missus?" the first man asked, curiously.

Missourians! It had been a word to frighten Mormon children with ever since she could remember. She tugged on Daisy's rope, desperation straining her voice. "Come on, Daisy!"

The man held tight to Daisy's collar. "Possession's nine points of the law." The teasing brightness in his eyes was more troubling than reassuring.

Ellen pulled harder and Daisy bellowed protestingly at this tug-of-war.

A new voice spoke. "It's her cow. Give it to her."

Ellen turned her head and saw that the tall boy with the yellow hair who had walked into the firelight with an armful of wood was the same who had slipped the dried peach into her hand at Brother Atkins' store.

He was much younger than she had assumed in the dusky interior of the store. She saw now that though his shoulders were as broad as those of the big bearded man, he had the thinness of a boy recently grown to man's height. He must be only a year or two older than herself.

"Who says she's her cow?" jeered the man holding Daisy. "I ain't seen any proof yet."

The boy dropped his armload of wood. "I'll prove it for her if you don't let that critter go."

The two men looked at him in surprise. The bearded one, who had squatted to turn his meat, set his skillet off the fire and straightened slowly. The fire blazed up, flickering on the boy's yellow hair as he stood tensely waiting.

For an instant they stood in a stiff triangle, the two older men on one side of Ellen and Daisy, the boy on the other. Then the smaller of the two men, the one with the weasel face, dropped his hand from Daisy's collar.

"Why, you young whelp!" he said, with such fury in his voice that Ellen drew back in fear. "I'll show you who's runnin' this fit-out!"

He went past Ellen in a rush, and something tightened in her heart as she saw the way the boy stood his ground, waiting. The boy's fist glanced off the man's head while the man's blow caught him squarely and sent him sprawling. Before he could rise the little man leaped on him like a cat.

But his big bearded companion reached them and plucked him off. "What do you think you're doing?" he growled. "Do you fight with children?"

"I'm no child!" the boy said, angrily, getting to his feet.

"I'm gonna thresh him, that's what I'm gonna do!" the little man said. "Jest let me show him who's runnin'—"

"*I'm* runnin' this fit-out," the big man said, calmly. "We don't want a cow, nohow. She'd slow us down too much. Take your critter and git home," he told Ellen.

He turned to the boy. "We don't want trouble, neither. You better take your b'longin's and clear out, Chris."

CHAPTER 4

ELLEN drew a deep breath and pulled on the rope.
Daisy tossed her head with a roll of her eyes and
a gentle protest, but fell into a walk behind her. They
crossed the circle of firelight in a waiting silence
broken only by the movements of the boy Chris, as he
gathered his belongings.

By the time Ellen entered the cottonwoods he was
at Daisy's heels. Behind them she heard the man who
had knocked him down mutter, "And good riddance!"

In answer the boy began whistling a jaunty tune,
and Ellen was filled with admiration for his spirit. She
turned around to smile at him and saw the stick over
his shoulder with the bundle knotted and hanging from
it.

"Going toward the settlement?"

"Yes, and I'll be glad for your company," Ellen said,
gratefully. "I can't thank you enough. You don't know

23

how important Daisy is to us. We'd sore miss her."

"I figured they'd stolen that little cow," he said, catching up with her, "even if they did claim she was wandering around loose."

"She probably did pull her stake," Ellen admitted, "but she would have come home. Joey—he's my brother —is supposed to herd her, move her stake when the grass is gone and bring her in before dark. But he's only ten and—" She hesitated.

"I know," he agreed. "Sort of careless, like a boy will be."

She could not help wondering what he had been doing with the Missourians, for so she thought of them. "They're not kin of yours?" she asked, anxiously.

"Those men?" He gave a derisive snort. "I fell in with them two days back. I want to get to California and that's where they're headed. But I aim to find better traveling companions here on the river. I'm going to the gold fields. A fellow can make a start there—"

"Or be killed by Indians!" Ellen said, bitterly.

He looked curiously at her. "I guess the real reason I've such a hankerin' to go to California is because my father's out there. I haven't seen him since I was knee-high to a grasshopper, but I know I'll find him in the gold fields. He'd be one of the first there."

"My father was one of the first in the gold fields," Ellen began, then stopped, drawing a long shuddering breath.

Chris asked, "What's the matter?"

"He—isn't coming back." The reality of her loss had just come home to her. They were alone now, she and Joey and Mama.

"Why not?" The boy's matter-of-factness helped her steady her voice.

"He stayed to work in California after the war ended."

"He was a soldier?"

She said proudly, "He was in the Mormon Battalion."

"Mormons, eh?" Chris said, with a sidewise glance at her. "Then you haven't all gone out to the Salt Lake Valley with Brigham Young."

"My father planned to return here for us." Her voice choked down, but she told him all of it—the cruel arrows, and the stolen gold dust that was to have paid for their fit-out for the trip west. It was a relief to speak of it.

"I'm glad those ruffians didn't get away with your cow," Chris said when she finished, and she felt cheered. She remembered the way Chris had picked himself up off the ground and come away whistling, and wished she had his spunk.

The night had lost its loneliness. Ellen could see a spatter of stars. She stopped pulling so hard on Daisy's rope and began listening to the song of the frogs in the marshy places around them.

When they neared the dugout, still talking, with Daisy's bell clanking comfortably behind them, Ellen heard someone say, "There she is now!" and the door was thrown open, letting out a simultaneous burst of candlelight and sound.

The small room was filled with her mother's friends. Through the door she glimpsed Sister Sarah's red head and the kind, lined face of Sister Andrews, just behind tall, black-bearded Brother Safford and his frail wife. Several assorted children were asleep on the bunk in view. Across the room she could see her mother, her face still pale and blank, rocking back and forth in the little cherry rocker by the fire.

Joey came through the door with a bucket and silently took Daisy's rope from her. There were tear-streaks on his face. He wouldn't get much milk tonight, Ellen wanted to tell him.

The Saffords were just leaving and Brother Safford looked sharply at Chris, behind Ellen in the doorway. Hurriedly, Ellen explained his presence.

"So you're on your way to California," Brother Safford said, his black eyes piercing Chris. "Can you handle a team of oxen?"

"Yes, sir."

"Come to see me in the morning. I'm going to the Salt Lake Valley in a few weeks and I need another teamster."

"Where will I find you?"

"A short walk north of the Log Tabernacle. Ask anyone where Phineas Safford's cabin stands."

"Thank you, sir." Chris turned to smile at Ellen, who was vainly trying to get her mother's attention. "Good night," he said, and walked off into the darkness.

"I must get on home, too," Sister Andrews was saying. She looked down at the dirt floor of the dugout and shivered. "Sister Harriet, wouldn't you like to have our little log house when we leave? You would be so much more comfortable there. It's small, but it's floored and weather-tight."

"Thank you, Sister Emma," Harriet Barlow said, mechanically, "but we won't need it. We shall be crossing the plains very soon now ourselves."

"Oh, I'm so glad!" Sister Andrews said, but her kind eyes flew to her husband's in perplexity, and Ellen looked at her mother in astonishment.

There was a gathering up of sleeping children, a shaking of hands and a muted confusion of good-bys.

"Joey!" Ellen's mother called. "Where's Joey? Ellen, ask him to see Sister Sarah home with the lantern."

"Joey's milking."

"The stars are out, Sister Harriet. I can find my way."

"We'll see Sister Sarah home," Brother Andrews said. "Good night, Sister Harriet."

"Good night—good night."

When the dugout was emptied, Ellen turned to her mother. "You told them we were going across the plains!"

"There is no reason to wait here any longer," her mother said, bleakly. "We must gather with the Saints." There was a faraway look in her eyes. "Sister Emma has promised me some of her zinnia seeds. We'll take some with us."

Ellen stared in disbelief. Her mother spoke as if it

were settled they should make the journey. But how could they? The wagon in which they had left Nauvoo, as well as the oxen, had long since been sold to others crossing the plains ahead of them in return for desperately needed food.

"We owe Brother Atkins—" Ellen stopped, not wishing to tell her mother how the storekeeper had grumbled about their account this afternoon.

"That reminds me," Harriet Barlow said. "I must ask Brother Atkins for a cholera remedy to take with us."

Flower seeds and a cholera remedy! When they needed a good stout wagon, at least four oxen, and provisions for several months in order to make the journey!

"It was your father's plan, you know," Harriet Barlow reminded her daughter, aware at last of Ellen's consternation.

"But I just don't see how—" Ellen began, in a choked voice.

"The Lord will provide a way," her mother said, vaguely, taking down her long dark hair to braid it for the night.

A dozen reminders sprang to Ellen's lips—that they had no money and no prospect of paying their debt, that even if the Lord provided a wagon and oxen they had no driver, that here on the Missouri they at least had a dirt roof over their heads—but she had the frightening conviction that right now her mother would not hear a word she said. She went to the fire and dished up a helping of stew.

Joey came in with his bucket half full of milk. Ellen said, "I'll strain it, Mama," and went to the chest for a clean square of factory.

They were in bed, Joey in one bunk and she and her mother in the other, when Ellen remembered that Chris had been ordered out of the Missourians' camp without his supper.

Shame for her thoughtlessness filled her. And where would he sleep tonight, with all his belongings on a stick thrown across his shoulder, and snow and mud still on the ground?

"Mama?" she said, softly.

Her mother did not reply, and yet Ellen was sure she was not asleep. She wondered if her mother were remembering that hot July day the Battalion marched away while Brother Pitt's band played *The Girl I Left Behind Me.*

Through the chinked logs she could hear Daisy stirring restlessly in the straw of her willow shelter a few feet away. Daisy gave a low protesting bellow, and Ellen thought, "There's someone out there!"

Then she realized it must be Chris. Quietly she slid from the bed and pulled on her clothing. In the red glow from the banked fire she found a loaf of bread and a spoon and the bowl into which she had scraped the left-over stew.

When she slid back the wooden bolt and let herself out of the dark dugout into the starlit night she could see clearly the way to the lean-to shelter.

As quietly as she moved, Chris had heard her coming. He sprang up from the straw to watch her approach. "It's you."

"I've brought you some supper." Unconsciously they were both whispering.

"You needn't have troubled."

She sniffed the smell of warm milk as she came nearer, and she could not help laughing. "You will never go hungry, will you, Chris?"

He laughed with her, not at all embarrassed. "Daisy had not much supper left for me, tonight."

Ellen handed him the bowl of stew and the bread. "When I was little I used to stand beside my father when he milked and open my mouth as wide as I could. 'Look at the greedy bird!' he'd say. 'Can't wait for her supper!'"

She was silent a moment, her heart overflowing with memories. "I always thought it was such fun when he missed my mouth. I didn't guess for a long time that he missed on purpose sometimes, just to tease me."

Chris had squatted in the doorway of the lean-to. Ellen leaned against an upright pole and watched him eat, thinking that he must be famished.

Presently he put the bowl down with a satisfied sigh. "Good old Daisy," he said, patting a velvety flank. "I'm sure glad she pulled her stake tonight." But his smiling eyes told Ellen he meant his gratitude for her.

She smiled back at him. "The Saffords will be better company crossing the plains."

"I wonder how those two daughters of his will like living in a prairie schooner?" Chris said, with a grin.

Their eyes met in shared amusement. Without his saying more Ellen knew he too had thought the Safford girls a little persnickety in the store this afternoon.

"I wish you were going, Ellen."

She sat down with her back against the pole. "Mama says we're going. She's dead set on it," she confided, worriedly, "and I don't see how we can get a fit-out together."

"How does your mother plan to do it?"

"I don't think she has a plan. Just a determination. She says, 'The Lord will provide a way.' "

Chris considered that, chewing reflectively on a long straw. "My father always said the Lord helps those who help themselves." His eyes were going over Daisy in a speculative way.

"We could trade Daisy-Very-Gently, I suppose," Ellen made herself say, over a lump in her throat. "It would be a hard trip for her, anyway."

Chris thought about that. "Might be, but she looks like a hardy little cow. And you'd have milk along the way. At least for a while."

He looked at Ellen. "What about that pretty little cherry rocker I saw? Would your mother part with it for some provisions?"

"I think so. I don't think she cares about anything else but getting to the Valley."

"We've got a few weeks to figure something out," Chris told her, and a wild hope began pounding in her. Could they really do it? "Maybe I'll think of something." Chris stretched contentedly. "Now for my featherbed—mine and Daisy's."

Ellen was still smiling when she let herself into the dugout. An odd clicking noise came from her mother's bunk. As Ellen drew near she realized her mother was sitting up in bed. "What are you doing, Mama?"

"Knitting."

"How can you see?"

"I don't need to see."

"It's getting late," Ellen said, uneasily. "Shouldn't you try to sleep?"

"There is so much to be done before we leave," her mother said, vaguely. "You and Joey will need heavy stockings—" Her whisper trailed off, but her needles clicked feverishly fast.

Ellen slipped into bed and listened from her pillow. "Mama, how much money will it take for the four months' provisions Brother Brigham insists every family have? And this time don't say the Lord will provide!"

"Have you so little faith?" her mother reproved her.

The Lord helps those who help themselves, Ellen reminded her silently. Her mother must have forgotten how her father had helped things along whenever they called on the Lord.

It was up to her now. The responsibility of attempting the dangerous, almost impossibly expensive journey across the plains to join the Saints lay heavily on her thin fifteen-year-old shoulders.

CHAPTER 5

HER mother was sleeping when Ellen wakened. She slid carefully out of bed in the darkness and went to stir up the fire, her feet arching away from the cold floor.

There had been no sound from Joey's bed, but in the flickering light that sprang up as the kindling she laid over the coals caught fire, she saw that her brother was awake, staring up at the stained factory ceiling. Ellen felt a pang of sympathy. Perhaps Joey missed their father most of all.

As she crawled back in bed, her mother stirred and said, sleepily, "Did you put some water on for the mush, Ellen?"

"Yes, Mama."

She was still wondering what she could say to take that sober look out of Joey's eyes when they were dressing before the fire. She dug into her skirt pocket and touched the dried peach Chris had given her. She had forgotten all about it!

On an impulse she brought it out and handed it to Joey, and was rewarded by the look of surprised pleasure that crossed his face. Chewing on it, he went out with the milk bucket. Ellen called after him, "Ask Chris in for breakfast."

"Chris? Who's Chris?"

"You'll see. He slept in the straw."

"Why'd he do that?"

"Oh, go along!" Ellen said, and pushed him outside.

She had already set four bowls of steaming mush at the table when Joey came back and reported there was nobody in the straw but Daisy. Ellen felt a prick of disappointment that the yellow-haired boy had not waited to bid them good-by.

After the breakfast dishes were washed and put away, the milk strained through clean squares of factory and set on the coolest shelf for the cream to rise, Ellen and her mother put on their Sunday dresses.

Harriet Barlow, looking pale but composed, wound her braided hair around her head. With fingers that trembled only a little, she pinned the Italian cameo that had belonged to Ellen's grandmother at her throat. Ellen thought with pride how handsome her mother looked.

When they were ready to leave the dugout they discovered that Joey had disappeared.

"I'll find him, Mama. Why don't you walk on with Sister Sarah and we'll meet you at the tabernacle?"

Her mother agreed, and Ellen left, hastening down the bluff toward the white tent city on the shore. The day was fine, and the inhabitants of the tent city were all out in the sunshine. Some were already strolling in the direction of the Log Tabernacle, others were dressing small children before their tents, and still others were washing up breakfast pots beside campfires.

New wagons and old, in all stages of preparation for the trip across the plains, stood about in the open spaces between the tents. A few over-eager men were using the Sabbath for painting and carpentering. Ellen examined their preparations with an intense and pointed interest.

Suddenly, a small furious upheaval of arms and legs came toward her around a canvas corner, tripped over a tent stake and rolled almost to her feet. Joey lay in the trampled mud looking up at her with a ludicrous expression of surprise.

Ellen grabbed him by his collar and lifted him to his feet. "Look at you!" she scolded him, her cheeks pink with annoyance.

The boy underneath him scrambled up and peered at her through an obstruction of dirty yellow hair that hung almost to his nose. His sharp-eyed scrutiny lasted all of a second. Then he shouted shrilly, " 'Ere! Give it me!" and snatched an India-rubber ball from Joey's hands, darting off again. Joey broke out of her grasp and ran after him, although Ellen stamped her foot and cried, "Joey! Joey! You come back here!"

A sharp-nosed woman with the same dirty color to

her hair stuck her head out of the tent. "W'ot is it now?" she inquired. "Oh, hello, miss!"

"I'm Joey's sister," Ellen explained. "I've come to take him to meeting, if he's still fit to go."

The two boys came streaking around the tent and the woman reached out a practiced hand and seized the small blond one by an ear.

" 'Ere, now, Bertie! That's no way to behave! Do you want me to box your ears for you?" She dropped her shrill voice a tone and said to Ellen, "They're fair demons together. I'm Liz Priddy. W'ot's your name?"

"Ellen Barlow."

"Who knits Joey's stockings, Ellen?"

"My mother."

"Would your mother 'ave a pair or two to sell?"

Ellen looked at her in wonder and joy, remembering her mother's furious knitting in the night. "Oh, I think so! I'll ask her."

"Thank you, dearie. Come 'ere, Bertie! We'll 'ave to 'ave another washup before you can go to church!"

As Ellen turned toward the tabernacle with Joey beside her, she wondered whether other English women would be willing to buy, and if fifty cents were too high a price.

The tabernacle was filled to overflowing, nearly a thousand Saints seated on its rough benches. Ellen sat beside her mother with Joey squeezed tightly between them and listened to the messages brought by the travelers from the Salt Lake Valley.

Brother Brewer spoke first, in an humble, matter-of-fact way. The Saints were well and happy, he told them, if a little hungry. It had been lean going during the winter, partly because of the lateness of planting the season before, and partly because of a plague of crickets which would have completely devoured the pioneers' first crop if God had not darkened the sky with the flapping wings of a miracle—thousands of sea-gulls sent to devour the crickets!

Brother Angell rose and said, with feeling: "I bring you greetings from our beloved brother, Brigham Young. I want to bring you his very words, as he spoke them to us in the Bowery on a cold day in February, when we stood shivering before him in our rags and homespun, some of us tempted in our poverty to go on to the gold mines of California."

His voice rose powerfully. " 'We have been kicked out of the frying pan into the fire,' Brother Brigham said, 'out of the fire into the middle of the floor, and here we are and here we will stay. God has shown me that this is the spot to locate his people, and here is where they will prosper ... He will rebuke the frost and the land shall become fruitful with the apple, peach and plum; yea, and the more delicate fruits, the strawberry and raspberry ... we will build towns and cities by the hundreds ... this will become the great highway of the nations ...' "

A sigh rippled over the congregation, breathed from a thousand throats. Ellen heard her mother's, full of a rapt yearning, but no more so than the nine hundred and ninety-nine others.

To the Valley! they all seemed to say. *Let us gather in the Valley.*

When Brother Angell sat down, another brother rose to read from a list of articles considered necessary for the journey across the plains.

It was something Ellen had heard before, but today she listened with tense attention.

"—for each family a good, well-covered wagon with two or three yoke of young oxen—milk cows, a beef and some sheep or pigs—one thousand pounds of flour, fifty pounds each of sugar, rice, bacon—thirty pounds of beans—"

Ellen's heart sank as the list lengthened.

"Musket, powder, lead, pepper, mustard, cinnamon, salt, saleratus, dried fruits, soap, fishhooks and lines, cooking utensils, a good tent—"

He reminded them of Brigham Young's counsel to bring with them seeds of every kind, and closed with Brother Brigham's exhortation to them not to forget the widows and the orphans in their preparations, but to help them to gather, too.

Three benches ahead of Ellen, Brother Atkins blew his nose. There was one person well able to help them and the least likely to do it, Ellen thought, fixing resentful eyes on the shiny bald back of his head.

Then she chided herself for harboring such thoughts in the Lord's tabernacle.

After the prayer the congregation rose and moved toward the door. Harriet Barlow paused to greet several friends, and one of them was saying, "—he sheared early because we're leaving with the first company. Those poor shivering ewes pull at my heart, so naked and thin! And I don't see how I can spin before we leave, there's so much else to be done."

Ellen spoke up in a rush. "Sister Garnett, I'll card and wash and spin your wool for half!"

She held her breath while they all looked at her and then at her mother, standing still with surprise. Then the sister said kindly, "Why didn't I think of that? I'll ask Brother Garnett to bring it to you tomorrow, Ellen."

"Thank you," Ellen said, her heart swelling.

After all, there were only three of them—they would not need so much!

CHAPTER 6

BROTHER GARNETT delivered the wool early the next morning, and Ellen soon had water heating in her mother's big wash pot. She and her mother both pitched in to wash the oily fleeces.

"Phew!" Joey cried, when he came back with an armful of wood. "Is there anything smells worse than wet wool?"

"Never mind that!" his mother said. "You'd better go after another load. We'll have to keep the fire going all day. Then you must help us string some lines for drying it. It's good it's a fine day." Her cheeks showed a little color for the first time since the news of her husband had come.

Joey left but he did not return with more wood, and there was no time to look for him. Ellen and her mother strung the lines and hoped the wood would last.

When the last wet woolly fleece was hung in the sun outside the dugout, it was well into afternoon and

Ellen's hands were red and swollen from the strong soap and the scratchy wool.

Her mother went to look for Joey who still had not returned. Ellen put on a fresh dress and made her way to the Saffords' cabin to see if she could borrow a small spinning wheel.

She had never seen so many strangers in the settlement. They milled in the road like bees crawling over and over one another in a hive. Many of them were headed for the gold fields. They were easily distinguishable from the Saints—rough, bearded men with fast little fit-outs pulled by horses or mules, and voices sharp with the excitement of preparation and their eagerness to be off. No seeds and plows in their light wagons that crowded the space before the blacksmith's shop and the tinshop!

The Saffords lived in a chinked log cabin at the north edge of the settlement. Behind the cabin was a crude barn and a large corral and, just visible, the white cover of a new Conestoga wagon.

Inside, Ellen found Sister Safford and her two daughters busy at dressmaking. The new sprigged muslin was unrolled on a clean sheet laid across the rough plank table. Diantha had her mouth full of pins. She waved a pair of scissors by way of greeting.

"What do you think of it?" Zina demanded. "They're to be cut just alike."

"It's beautiful," Ellen said, from her heart.

Sister Safford sat on a low chair, supervising. Ellen had never seen her when she did not look tired and pale, but her face had an expression of extraordinary sweetness. She had never recovered, Ellen's mother said once, from the exposures of that dreadful winter when they had all been forced to flee Nauvoo.

"I'm sure I don't know why the girls need new dresses for the plains," she said gently, smiling at Ellen.

Ellen explained her errand. When she mentioned Sister Priddy, who wanted to buy stockings, Sister Safford said with a troubled look, "Did you know there is cholera among the new converts, Ellen? I heard it yesterday at meeting. Some were stricken before they left the boat."

Ellen did not know, and the news disturbed her. Joey was probably down there at this moment.

"The California emigrants might buy from you," Sister Safford suggested. "There are so many of them passing through. Hardly a day passes but some of them come here trying to buy supplies for the journey."

"Do you know what they ask for?" Diantha put in. "Dried bread!"

"And factory sacks to carry it in," Zina added.

"They are in such a hurry to get to the gold mines they won't stop to cook along the trail," their mother said. "Thank heaven oxen are too slow for most of them, or Brother Safford would not be able to find his other team."

"Papa is out buying more oxen now," Zina told Ellen.

"Is your mother really planning to cross the plains this summer, Ellen?"

"She has her heart set on it, Sister Safford."

"Then she must have my little sheet iron campstove. Brother Safford has decided we will have room to take the step stove, and what a blessing it will be when we reach the Valley!" She glanced toward the corner where it stood, spreading a comfortable warmth. "Zina, take Ellen out to the shed and show her that little camp-stove. Its legs fold under for carrying."

"We'll be happy to have it," Ellen said quickly and gratefully.

"Come along, Diantha," Zina cried. "Let's show Ellen our new wagon."

Ellen told Sister Safford good-by and followed the two girls outside. The big wagon stood in the back yard, its new canvas sharply white, the bed fresh with paint of a pleasing dark green.

Ellen heard a jaunty whistle and spotted a familiar yellow head in the corral beyond the wagon. Chris was driving two yoked oxen round and round the corral, shouting cheerfully at them although it did not look to be an easy task. The oxen pulled apart then ran their flanks together, stumbling a little in fright and clumsiness, obviously not accustomed to the heavy wooden yoke.

The Safford girls paid no attention but Ellen waved as he came around. They scrambled up over the wheel into the wagon and Ellen followed them.

Inside, two chests were already nailed solidly in place with a space left for the stove. One was for provisions, the girls explained, and the other for clothing.

"The featherbeds will go on top," Zina said. "Mama will sleep on one and Diantha and I on the other. The menfolks will sleep in a tent."

"Mama is too frail to walk the whole way," Diantha said, "so she is to have her little chair right here."

"It's like a house on wheels," Ellen cried admiringly.

"Everyone else must walk," Zina said, her dark cheeks colored with excitement. "There will be another wagon, but it must carry our household things, the china and pieces of furniture Mama wants with her. We're to have two Conestogas with three yoke of oxen for each," she boasted.

"That's besides the church wagons Papa is to have charge of," Diantha explained. "That's why he had to hire teamsters, first Tom Bedford and now this new one, Chris Denham. Charles and Hyrum will drive our wagons." Charles and Hyrum were their two brothers.

Zina giggled. "Shall I tell you who's sweet on Diantha? You'd never guess!"

"Hush!" Diantha said, faint color coming under her porcelain skin. "Don't you dare tell!"

"Oh, all right, silly! Look, Ellen, this is where the flour barrel will stand."

Crossing the plains was like an outing to them, Ellen realized listening to their chatter. And perhaps it would be an outing, fitted out so fine. She looked at everything with an envy she tried hard to hide.

When she had admired everything and inspected the little sheet iron stove, the girls told her good-by and went back to their dressmaking. Ellen lingered near the corral until Chris came around once more.

When he saw she was alone he called, "I've got something to show you, Ellen." He looped his long line around a pole and jumped over the fence. The oxen looked after him incuriously.

"Will they stand?" Ellen asked.

Chris laughed. "They're glad for a rest." He beckoned her to follow him. "Look at that!" he said. Behind the shed stood a small worn wagon about half the size of the Conestoga. She regarded it silently.

Chris glanced at her face. "It doesn't look like much," he agreed, "but with new tires from the blacksmith and some bows from the wheelwright to hold a canvas cover I think it would make the journey. It is light enough so that Daisy and an ox could draw it. It would hold your provisions and a few things besides."

If I hadn't seen the Saffords' wagon first! Ellen thought.

"Mr. Safford doesn't plan to use it," Chris told her. "You might be able to buy it if he doesn't let some California emigrant trade him out of it."

"It's just what a California emigrant would want," Ellen agreed.

"I'm sure he would rather sell it to you and your mother. If you could be ready when we leave."

Ellen shook her head. "I never realized until yesterday how many things we will need. All Mama's friends want to help but most of them are just like us, poor as Job's turkey and yearning with all their hearts to gather with the Saints."

Chris laughed. "If wishes were wings the whole settlement of Kanesville would just up and fly to the Salt Lake Valley!"

Ellen did not laugh. "Anybody that's been homeless

as long as we have," she said fiercely, "would yearn for a place to settle."

"You'll get there."

"If I can get some flour I am going to bake bread and slice and dry it, and sell it to the California emigrants. Mama can sew factory sacks to carry it in."

"The storekeeper might advance you the flour and factory."

She shook her head. She could imagine just what the old storekeeper would say. *Come and talk to me when you've paid your bill, Ellen.*

"Ask him," Chris advised, smiling down into her troubled face.

On her way home Ellen passed the cabin where Brother Atkins and his wife lived. It boasted the only glass-paned window in Kanesville. Sister Atkins had a treasured lace panel hanging before it, but she had already lit her oil lamp and Ellen could see clearly through the lace.

As she watched, Brother Atkins came in from the other room, seated himself in the high-backed walnut chair under the lamp and picked up a Bible. The yellow light gleamed on his bald head and on his spectacles. She could think of nothing more difficult than asking the peppery old storekeeper for help, and she knew if she put it off until tomorrow it would be even harder.

She drew a deep breath and walked up to the cabin. All at once her heart was beating so hard she could hear it plainly. She forced herself to raise her hand and gave a soft, frightened knock on the door.

CHAPTER 7

THE ATKINS cabin had a real wood floor and she could hear plainly the steps crossing it to the door. It opened and Brother Atkins stood before her, blinking his eyes.

"Why, it's Ellen Barlow!" he said, his sour face screwing up in a smile. "Come in, my dear." He stepped back and, a little dazed by this reception, Ellen entered the cabin.

"We have a caller, Idy!" Brother Atkins called to his wife. His shirt was open and his neck looked scrawny as a plucked chicken's, but here in his own home he seemed a gentler man, not so forbidding.

He took off his spectacles and wiped them on a large white handkechief. "I'm glad you came, Ellen. I've been looking for an opportunity to ask your pardon."

Ellen looked up at him in amazement. Just then Sister Atkins hurried in, wiping her hands on her apron.

47

She was as tall as her husband and almost as thin, but her expression was pleasant and relaxed.

"Forgive me, dear, but I had my hands in my pie crust. I'm sorry about your father, Ellen. How is your mother taking it?"

"Pretty well, I think."

"I was just asking Ellen to pardon my bad temper the other day when she was in the store." Her husband shook his head ruefully. "Brother Brigham has often chid me about my temper. Sit down, Ellen."

Seated in a low rocker facing their unexpectedly kind faces, Ellen found it easy to tell them of her mother's obsession to join the Saints in the Valley, and of her plan to earn their provisions.

"Maybe I can help you, Ellen. I can't get enough hardtack to supply the emigrants who are stocking up at my store this spring. Why can't I sell your dried bread for you?"

She looked at him with shining eyes. "*Would* you?"

"I think I can handle all the rusk you can pack for me," he told her.

They talked on, settling the details. "After our bill is paid—"

"I will cancel your old bill, Ellen."

When she protested, he gave a dry cackle of a laugh. "Won't it cost me less to help you get to the Valley than to carry you on my books until Joey grows up or you marry a rich man?"

"Now, Daniel!" his wife chided him, and they both laughed as Ellen blushed.

She went home full of hope and wonder at the ways

of the Lord with those who dared the impossible. Suppose she had not found the courage to talk to Brother Atkins? She would never have known what he was really like!

Her ears still rang with his last words. "You're a brave girl, Ellen," he had told her at the door, blowing his nose with emotion. Her heart was as warm as the fresh-baked dried peach pie Sister Atkins had insisted on tucking into the extra bake pan she loaned her.

But when she reported the conversation to her mother, Harriet Barlow said with pink cheeks, "Certainly we'll pay our bill!"

"But, Mama—how?"

"The Lord will provide a way," her mother said firmly. "Hasn't He provided us with a way to earn the money?"

"Oh, *Mama!*" Ellen said, in loving exasperation.

The next weeks were busy ones. Ellen mixed and kneaded and baked tirelessly. While the loaves browned in the coals of the fire, she carded the wool and spun it into yarn which her mother knitted into stockings by night.

It was Joey's task to keep the wood box filled and to bring the sacks of flour and bolts of factory from Brother Atkins' store on his crudely fashioned sled. It was hard work pulling the wooden runners over bare earth, only possible because of the fresh new grasses sprouting everywhere, and Joey was rebellious.

One day, going to look for him when he had not returned from the store, Ellen came across the wagon-sled still loaded with sacks of sliced, dried bread, left unattended in the middle of the road before the wagon-maker's where the teams of oxen had to be driven around it.

She dragged it the long way to Brother Atkins, furious with the thought that some greedy gold-seeker could have had provisions for his journey for the taking, and robbed her of the pay for several days' work while Joey played tag with Bertie Priddy.

When Joey came in after dark Ellen exploded. He had been away all day and Daisy was still unmilked!

"Oh, Daisy can wait," Joey said, carelessly. "She's not going any place."

"And neither will we, for all you're doing!" Their mother had walked up the hill to see Sister Sarah, and so Ellen spoke her mind. "Mama and I are trying so hard, and you won't even see that Daisy is milked regularly so she won't dry up before we start our journey. What would Papa think of you?"

To her surprise Joey's eyes filled with tears. He flung away from her, trying to hide them, and threw himself face down on his bunk.

"Joey—Joey, I'm sorry," Ellen said, bending over him in distress.

"Keep away from me!" he cried, his voice muffled in the buffalo robe.

"But, Joey—"

"All right, all right, I'll milk her!" he cried, springing up. He pushed past her, grabbed up the bucket and rushed out of the dugout.

After that, for a while, Joey worked with them. But no matter how long and how hard they labored, the days were too short. They must mold a supply of candles and make soap. Spin. Mold. Bake. Knit. It was nearing time for Brother Safford's company to leave. Another company would leave three weeks later and a third three weeks after that. By that time it would be July and it was not safe to begin the journey much later.

Chris came to tell them good-by the night before the Saffords left for the rendezvous on the Elk Horn.

"Has he sold the little wagon?" Ellen asked, anxiously.

"Not yet. Can you buy it?"

Ellen sighed. "I haven't even had time to figure my accounts."

"Ellen and I go at a trot all day," her mother told him. "We could have walked to the Valley in the steps we've taken these last weeks."

"You'll get there, ma'am."

"We'll see you in the Valley, I hope," Harriet Barlow said, pleasantly.

Ellen and Chris exchanged a look. "No, ma'am, I'll be pushing on to California as soon as I can. I wish you a successful journey." His eyes sought Ellen's again. "I wish we were traveling together."

She looked at his longish face under the lock of fair hair with a strangely heavy sensation around her heart. Would she ever see Chris Denham again?

"You'll find your father, Chris," she said, because she knew that would mean a successful journey to him.

"Thank you, Ellen." He shook hands gravely with Joey, which Ellen knew delighted her brother, and made her and her mother a little salute. Ellen knew she would miss him sorely.

After the supper things were put away, she sat at the table with the candle at her elbow and added her columns of figures. If Brother Safford took his light wagon with him, where would she find another? The wagon-maker wanted nigh a hundred dollars for a good stout wagon fitted with bows and a double cover, and a bucket of tar under the seat thrown in.

Joey sat across the table from her doing his lessons, for he went twice a week to the cabin of a young woman who had started a school. Her mother was in her little cherry rocker by the fire, knitting. There was a sharp knock at the door and Joey jumped up to open it.

Charlie Safford stood there, his young face pale and sober. "Sister Barlow, Pa wants to know if you can come back with me. Ma's took bad. We think it's the cholera."

"Oh, not the cholera!" Harriet said, like a prayer. "Not Sister Eliza! She's so frail—!" She stood up, dropping her knitting on her chair. "Ellen, run quick and ask Brother Atkins if he will open the store and give you some things for my remedy."

She was checking her shelf while Ellen lit the candle in the lantern. "I've got paregoric—camphor—we're not out of flour?" she asked, not stopping to uncover the barrel.

"No, Mama."

"Tell him I need charcoal—molasses—a little laudanum—I've got cayenne—"

Ellen threw a shawl over her shoulders and hurried out and through the darkness, swinging the lantern wildly. Shame flooded her for the quick thought that had come, making her heart leap. Now Brother Safford would not be able to start for the rendezvous in Omaha country in the morning! His journey would have to be postponed at least until the next company left. Chris would not be leaving for another three weeks, and in three weeks anything could happen. She might even be ready to go, too!

On the third morning Harriet Barlow came home, riding sidesaddle in front of Charlie on his father's big bay mare.

"Pa says your ma has the gift of healing," he told Ellen, jumping off to help her mother down. "If it wasn't for her we'd have lost Ma."

When he had ridden off, Ellen followed her mother into the dugout and went back to kneading her dough at the table, reluctant to lose a precious minute.

Her mother sat on the edge of their bunk, unbuttoning her shoes. "Brother Safford has given us a wagon for the journey."

Ellen leaned on her fists in the dough. "*Mama!*" she breathed.

Her mother sighed and stretched out on the bed. "It's small but strong. He thinks it will take us."

The little wagon Chris had shown her! "Of course, it will!" Ellen cried, happily.

"He included a yoke and harness. He says if we can be ready to leave with the July company he will look out for us on the journey."

"Will Sister Eliza be ready to travel?"

"Brother Phineas says we cannot leave later. It will probably be the last company this season. Even so, we will risk a snowstorm in the mountains."

Her mother's eyes closed in weariness and Ellen knew from the little noises of her breathing that she had fallen fast asleep. She kneaded faster and faster in her excitement. We *will* be ready, we *must* be ready, we *will*, we *must*—faster and faster until she had to stop to catch her breath.

She began shaping the dough into loaves, her heart singing. See how the way opened up! Her mother had been right to trust in the Lord.

But so was Chris right, Ellen thought, warmly. Because it was after they had begun helping themselves that the Lord had opened the way.

Now the days were not long enough. Chris repainted the little wagon and the blacksmith re-tired it in return for some of Harriet Barlow's chinaware. The wagon-maker equipped it with hoops and a canvas cover to repay Ellen's mother for her midwifery when his son was born. Ellen learned that Sister Eliza coveted her mother's little cherry rocker for her wagon, and persuaded her mother to trade it to the Saffords for a supply of bacon and dried beef to add to their provisions.

Light as the little wagon was, Daisy-Very-Gently could not pull it alone. From everyone she met Ellen inquired anxiously for an ox to team with Daisy, but no one had an animal to spare.

One day as she was scraping the hot coals off her

bake pans to take some fresh bread from the fire Chris Denham rode up on the Saffords' mare, very excited.

"I've found your ox, Ellen!" he shouted.

"Where?"

"Get up behind me! We must hurry if we're to have him."

She turned her loaves out to cool, covered them with a clean square of factory and snatched her bonnet from the peg where it hung. She put her foot in the stirrup and Chris grasped her hand to help her swing herself up behind him on the horse. He spurred the mare and she put her arms around him and hung on as they galloped off.

As they rode he told her he had come across some California emigrants who were in a fever of haste to reach the gold fields and would have to leave a lame ox.

"Will he be sound in time for our journey?" Ellen worried.

"We'll have to take that chance," Chris said. "Now don't let them rob you."

The emigrants' camp was south of Kanesville on a ridge above the river lowlands. Two rough-looking men were working to repair a broken harness while a young-ish woman stirred coffee just coming to a boil over the campfire. Nearby a man with drooping mustache was fussing gloomily over the lamed animal with a tobacco poultice.

Ellen hung behind Chris as he asked, "Is your critter any better?"

The man swore and spat.

"Going to leave him behind?" Chris persisted.

"What difference is it to you?"

"I think I can cure his lameness."

The heads of the other two gold-seekers came up and one of them asked dourly, "Afore morning?"

"No," Chris said. "Reckon it'll take about a week."

There were more oaths. Ellen put her hands over her ears, but the woman at the fire paid no attention.

"Maybe we can make a trade," Chris suggested.

"Not unless you got a horse or a mule."

Ellen spoke up. "I have a cherry chest, with carved legs."

The woman looked up from the fire, but the men laughed. "Child, we'll not burden ourselves with furnishings," one of them said. "What else have you got?"

"I've got dried bread, sacked for the journey." Reluctantly, she offered it. She had hoped to keep all she baked now for themselves.

Chris began dickering over amounts and in the end one of the men accompanied them home, leading the lame animal and a mule equipped with a pack sack in which to carry back the rusk.

When the man had loaded his provisions and left, Chris and Ellen tried to bed the ox down in Daisy's lean-to, but the little cow had a mind of her own about who should share her straw and made such a fuss that Ellen's mother and Joey came running out to see what the trouble was.

"Is this the ox that is to take us to the Valley?" her mother reproached Ellen when she saw the brindled animal. "He's badly lamed."

"But, Mama," Ellen said, anxiously, "everyone says

you have the gift of healing. Couldn't you heal an ox?"

Harriet Barlow gave her daughter a strange look. Then she laughed softly, putting an arm around Ellen's thin shoulders. "Why not?"

Finally, they hobbled Daisy and staked her outside the shelter so the lame ox, which they named Buff, could have a comfortable bed. Ellen's mother brewed a solution in which they soaked his foot.

"As soon as he can walk on it we must yoke him with Daisy so he can train her," Chris told Ellen. "Who will drive them for you?"

"If only we could find someone like you who would drive our oxen for a way to the Valley!"

"You would have to provide for him," Chris reminded her, "and a husky teamster could double the provisions necessary for your trip." He was looking her up and down in a curious way. "Do you think you could do it, Ellen?"

"*Me?*"

"You're little, but you've got the spunk for it."

Could *she* drive a team across a thousand miles of prairie and mountains? It was a man's job!

"I'll teach you what I know. And I can help you yoke and unyoke."

If she didn't do it, who would? Ellen drew a deep breath. "I'll do it, Chris."

"Good girl," he said, and went off, whistling.

The new ox rested well, but all that night they had to listen to Daisy's mournful complaints at being put out of her straw.

CHAPTER 8

A<small>T</small> last the day came. The little wagon was loaded
and Daisy and Buff yoked and hitched. Ellen
went into the dugout for one last look around—at the
bed frames bare of their buffalo robes, the stained factory ceiling through which the dirt of the roof had
sometimes sifted down on them, and the rude door
sagging on its leather hinges. Already it had the look
of an abandoned cave.

At the last moment Harriet Barlow's friends had
come, pressing gifts on her. A sister brought some carefully dried seed of the sweet wild strawberries she had
gathered, as fine as dust and more precious to her than
gold. A neighbor brought a short-handled shovel to
tie on the outside. Brother Lee who had the tinshop
brought a huge brass kettle for their wash and that was
tied outside the wagon, too, along with an ax for fire-

wood, the lantern and various cooking utensils and kegs.

"It looks like a peddler's wagon!" Ellen's mother cried, her cheeks glowing with excitement. And indeed it did.

The company was to ferry the Missouri at a point north of Kanesville. Sister Sarah and her husband, a big man with a chest like a flour barrel and a beard as flaming as his wife's hair, invited Ellen to follow their wagon through the settlement.

Chris had come over to help her yoke Daisy and Buff and get them started. Ellen took the long teamster's rope from him with misgivings.

"Hike!" she cried, and the cow and the ox fell in step behind the Stewart wagon, all the dangling pots and kegs clanking against the wagon.

"Keep them moving and you'll be all right," Chris called after her, as he turned toward the Safford cabin.

The morning was fine. Dew sparkled like fallen stars in the dusty grasses. Harriet sang softly as she walked beside Ellen. Joey, chockful of mischief, darted from one side of the wagon to the other, impatient of its slow progress.

"Joey, for heaven's sake!" Ellen finally cried out, in exasperation, "you're right under their hooves!"

He made a sassy face at her and slapped Buff's rump. The ox started and Daisy made a protesting sound as the yoke bit into her neck. She tossed her head and Buff bellowed angrily. Joey laughed and ran forward to join the Stewart children.

"Hi-i-yike!" Ellen shouted, and the animals settled to the yoke again.

There was a freedom in knowing all their possessions were beside them in the wagon and that the road to the Valley stretched ahead of them, sunny and inviting, with companionship along the way. She opened her mouth and joined her mother in song.

And then Daisy-Very-Gently stopped. Not all of Ellen's pleadings nor her mother's scoldings could persuade the little cow to lift a dainty hoof. She had made up her mind about the heavy yoke and the burden always at her heels, and that was that.

The Stewarts disappeared behind a clump of cottonwoods. Presently Joey came back, yelling, "Hey, what's the matter?"

Behind them in the road another wagon came to a stop and then another, until Ellen could see a line of them, all waiting on Daisy. She could feel her face growing hot.

From way back came a faint shout: "Giddyup, thar! Let's git movin'!"

"What's the matter, girlie?" the man behind her yelled. "Can't you drive?"

Even her mother was crying, "Ellen, can't you do something?"

She grew desperate and began switching Daisy's legs. The cow rolled her eyes and jerked backward. Buff plunged and between them they pulled the wagon half off the road. There they stopped again.

"Giddup! Giddup!" Ellen screamed, but they bawled

their stubborn defiance and would not move another inch.

Growing impatient, the man behind pulled around them. Soon the other waiting wagons followed him. Ellen could do nothing but wait, choking in their dust. Her mother had retired a clean distance from the road into a grassy field.

When the last wagon had passed, Joey let out a wild Indian war whoop. The startled animals plunged completely off the road, narrowly missing Harriet as they ran off across the grassy clearing.

Such a terrific clatter the brass pot and the shovel made, banging against the wagon! The lantern flew off and rolled over and over. Next the brass pot went sailing, ringing like a bell when it hit the ground.

Ellen went a-flying at the end of her long rope, too slight to slow the oxen down but exerting enough pull to keep them running in a circle. Behind them Harriet Barlow ran, crying, "Whoa! Whoa!" and trying to gather up the things that were scattering over the meadow. In the center of the circle Joey jumped up and down in excitement, screeching, "I started 'em! I started 'em!"

Ellen could hear laughter from the wagons going around the cottonwoods, but she was too busy to think about the ludicrous sight they must be.

Someone was running across the meadow toward them, shouting, *"Whoa!"* Miraculously the animals slowed and came to a stop with the wagon still upright.

It was Chris, who had come up with the Safford wagons. He had left his own triple yoke of oxen standing in the road. Ellen looked at him in gratitude, too out of breath to speak.

The sun seemed very hot indeed now. She was drenched with perspiration and her loosened hair was falling about her shoulders. Her own face flamed, but her mother looked pale and quite ill with exhaustion as she caught up, her arms full of the things she had gathered up.

Chris gently took Harriet's arm and made her sit down in the shade of the wagon while he tied on the lantern and the dented pots. Ellen poured her mother a drink from the water keg.

"Oh, dear," Harriet said, loosening the ties of her bonnet. "I'm afraid I can't go on."

"Mama!" Ellen said in consternation. "Not go on—to *Zion?*"

"I'm sorry," her mother said faintly. "I don't see how I can."

"Get up in the wagon and ride, ma'am," Chris told her. "Come on, Ellen, I'll help you back on the road."

A smart black buggy had pulled up behind Chris's wagon in the road. Ellen looked at the bearded man dismounting from it with feelings of dismay.

"I didn't know Brother Safford had a buggy like that."

"He hired it to take the womenfolk to the rendezvous," Chris told her.

In the buggy with their mother, looking cool and

morning fresh in their starched sunbonnets, sat Zina and Diantha.

"Where's Sister Harriet?" Brother Safford said sharply as he strode up.

"I'm all right, Brother Phineas," her mother called from the wagon, and her voice did sound stronger. "It was just a stitch in my side from running."

"Sister Harriet, you ride into camp with Sister Eliza. I'll take your wagon, Chris, and you drive Ellen's team in. Zina can drive the buggy."

It was all arranged in no time under Brother Safford's firm guidance. Ellen watched, disheveled and uncomfortably warm, as Zina coolly lifted the reins and guided the span of horses around her father's three yoke of oxen and trotted them smartly down the road. Brother Safford started up his wagon and Chris soon had Daisy and Buff following docilely in its dust.

Ellen trudged along beside him in silence, heartsick with worry and humiliation, but Chris whistled a little tune. "It will be easier tomorrow," he said cheerfully, after a little while. "You can do it, Ellen."

"I hope so," Ellen said, but she was not at all sure.

When they came to the river a long train of wagons waited their turn at the ferry. Ellen took her place in line and she and her mother unyoked Daisy and Buff, for word had been passed that the animals would have to swim.

Afterward, Ellen walked forward to the river. A scene of wild confusion met her eyes. Downstream from the ferry about two hundred oxen had entered the water. The leaders, panic-stricken when the current swept them into deep water, were turning and trying to fight their way back to shore. Milling and tossing their horns, the animals behind them were trying desperately to keep their heads above water, for to go under in the crush of red bodies meant certain drowning.

Men on horseback were shouting as they rode up and down the banks, whipping forward those still in shallow water. Others threw stones at the panicky leaders. Ellen searched anxiously for Daisy. The little cow was in deep water, her eyes rolling in terror.

A shout went up. Several women screamed. Ellen scrambled up a wagon wheel for a better view over the heads of the collecting crowd. A slim boy, his yellow hair gleaming in the sun, was out on the river, clambering barefoot over the oxen's backs!

It was Chris!

Her heart almost stopped as she watched him make his way from back to back, somehow evading the tossing horns, until he was astride the leader, hitting him on the sides of the head to guide him across the stream.

"Isn't that Papa's new teamster?" she heard a light amazed voice ask, and saw the Safford girls standing not far away. They were looking at Chris as if they had never seen him before, their faces alight with excitement and admiration.

Closing her eyes, Ellen said a little prayer for his safety. When she looked again, he was midway of the river, right in the swift current. The animals were swimming strongly now and spreading out. The riders plunged their horses into the water, herding the stragglers into line. A cheer went up from the watchers on the bank.

Meanwhile, using docile double spans of oxen on each bank, other men were loading and unloading the wagons as the ferry moved back and forth across the river. After a wait of more than two hours Ellen and her mother and Joey found themselves on the ferry, crossing the wide, swift-moving waters to the other side.

As they were yoking the animals again, Bertie Priddy came running again by. "It's a gypsy cart, that's w'ot it is!" he screeched, pointing at their wagon.

" 'Tis not!" Joey declared, torn between insult and amusement. His friend ran off, taunting, "Gypsies! Gypsies!"

Ellen pretended not to hear the laughter that followed the little English boy, but she was aware of the critical glances some of the men gave her fit-out.

When they reached the campground, Ellen had to have help in maneuvering her wagon into its place in the big ragged circle. That done, there was still the unyoking, and the animals to be fed and watered and turned out to graze before she could have her own supper.

There were many wagons already camped here, waiting for the full train to form. Here the company would be organized, with a captain for each ten wagons, and captains of fifties over them in authority.

The mood of the camp was one of gaiety and celebration, for everyone was happy to be started on the road to the Valley. When the supper campfires died down, a huge bonfire was built in the center of the circle of wagons, blazing high as a log cabin. A tall, bony brother came out of his wagon with a fiddle and struck up a lively tune.

Ellen lay on her stomach on the buffalo robes and watched through the parted wagon-cover, too tired from her first day's teamstering to join the dancers.

She saw Diantha and Zina Safford, wearing the new sprigged muslins, speak to Chris and she could imagine they were complimenting him on the way he swam the cattle across the river. Their faces were eager and friendly and they looked so pretty and fresh that Ellen felt a pang of jealousy. She was grimy and dusty and just too bone-weary to clean herself up.

While the fiddler played and the shadowy figures moved between her and the firelight with a flirting of skirts and a stamping of feet, she lay on her buffalo robes and soberly looked into the future.

They had a thousand miles to go, on foot. A hundred days like today! Their wagon was light and their team ill-matched. Had she and her mother and Joey the strength and courage to go on—or should they give up now and return to Kanesville? Her mother had been ready to quit this afternoon.

She thought of the dugout with its hard dirt floor and the dust that sifted down from the ceiling. She thought of the mountains of loaves of bread she had baked in the last weeks, of the wild ride she had taken behind Chris to find Buff. . . .

The Valley of the Mountains. Even in her mind the words made music. . . .

No. They would not go back . . . With the firelight playing on her dust-streaked cheeks, she fell asleep.

CHAPTER 9

ELLEN was wakened by a strange rumpus. She poked her head through the lapped edges of canvas and saw a young boy herding a flock of geese past her wagon. They were flapping their yellow bills in noisy outrage as they waddled ahead of his willow switch, and their awkward haste was so ludicrous that Ellen burst out laughing.

The boy looked up, startled, then laughed back.

The sun was up and the sky pale blue and cloudless. Spiraling wisps of gray marked a dozen or more campfires and the smell of woodsmoke mingled with frying bacon was delicious on the morning air.

Joey was sleeping, his lashes long against his cheek, his mouth slightly parted. He looked very young when he was asleep. Her mother was snoring lightly, the way she did when she was very tired.

Ellen dressed and went to see how the animals had

fared during the night. She found Buff not far away, grazing contentedly with a small herd of oxen, but Daisy was not among them.

As Ellen walked around the large circle she absorbed the sights and sounds of the wakening camp—the Stewart family kneeling in morning prayer, their bowed heads making an orange halo around their campfire—a man trimming his beard before a mirror propped against a wagon bow—a woman singing a hymn softly as she gathered eggs from an ingenious hens' nest slung from her wagon.

Ellen came around a wagon and saw ahead of her Bertie Priddy's yellow-haired mother with her arms akimbo, facing a portly man.

"I'll cook your breakfast, Brother Priddy, but I'll not milk your new cow!"

"But she's used to a woman, my darling. She kicked my bucket over last night for no reason but that I was wearing trousers."

"Then put on a skirt!"

"I'll do it, woman, if you'll get me one!" he roared.

Sister Priddy spun on her heel and climbed in their wagon while Ellen and a few neighbors watched, fascinated. Presently a flounced skirt came sailing out of the wagon.

Brother Priddy pulled the skirt up over his trousers and, picking up his milk bucket, cautiously approached the staked brindle cow. The cow looked over her shoulder at the man's flat-crowned hat and beard, and kicked up her heels.

"Fetch me a bonnet, Lizzie!" Brother Priddy bawled.

A calico bonnet flew out of the wagon, and Ellen and the others laughed. Muttering angrily, the man tied the bonnet under his beard and picked up his bucket again.

This time the cow looked at him curiously and turned away. The man knelt on one knee and began awkwardly sending thin streams of milk into his bucket. The sun was climbing. Perspiration trickled down Brother Priddy's cheeks. He pushed back the bonnet just as the brindle cow turned her head to look at him. When she saw his beard she kicked over the bucket and sent Brother Priddy sprawling.

Ellen joined in the hearty laughter as the enraged man, stumbling over the flounce on his wife's skirt, began chasing the cow around her stake, flailing her with the empty bucket.

She walked on. She met several children driving cows and oxen toward camp, but none had seen a Jersey cow with a white star on her forehead.

She turned toward the thicket of trees down on the creek bed. It was only a small thicket and there was a leafy stillness when she entered it. The cow would not be in here, Ellen thought, or she would have heard her bell.

In the very next moment she pushed aside a heavy willow branch and found herself looking Daisy in the face through a lacy screen of leaves. Girl and animal stared at each other.

Daisy-Very-Gently had been hiding from her! She

must have been standing very still, clever enough not even to chew her cud so that not the smallest tinkle would escape from her bell.

"Aren't you ashamed?" Ellen scolded her. But the look in the little cow's soft brown eyes disturbed her. Daisy wanted no part of being yoked to the wagon again and in her heart Ellen could not blame her. She picked up the rope and led the little cow back to camp.

When breakfast was over, Brother Safford and several other men came by inspecting the wagons. Chris followed them and Ellen told him the story of Daisy's hiding place in the willows. They all laughed.

"She's a bright little cow," Chris said.

The men walked around the wagon, looking doubtful. One of them poked at the wooden yoke, where it lay on the ground, with the toe of his boot.

"This puts more'n half the weight on the cow, don't it? Can't blame her for lightin' out."

The other eyed Ellen speculatively. "Nothin' but trouble here, Brother Safford."

"We must think of the good of the whole company," the first said pointedly.

A flush darkened Brother Safford's face and Harriet Barlow's cheeks turned an angry pink.

Chris broke a small embarrassed silence. "D'you know, I think I could fashion a yoke that would balance the load better."

"No harm in trying," Brother Safford said, and turned briskly away.

Ellen looked after them. "They don't think I can do it, do they, Mama?"

Her mother was still angry. "They're afraid we'll hold them back."

Chris was motioning urgently, excitement shining in his eyes. "Listen, Ellen, I saw a piece of black willow driftwood down on the bank. Let's go get it."

Ellen hurried after him, wondering what a piece of black willow the river had tossed up on the sand could do that the yoke they had already could not.

"I hope nobody's picked it up for firewood," Chris worried. He was at the river's edge ahead of her. "It's still here! Do you think we can lift it?"

She ran up beside him. The gnarled limb was half-buried in sand. It looked long and heavy. They knelt and began scooping sand with their hands. When it was partially uncovered, Chris took the small hatchet from his belt and chopped it in two. The end he had freed was curved almost like a question mark.

For the life of her Ellen couldn't see an ox yoke in it. But she cheerfully picked up one end of it, and they started back to camp. The sun was warm and a steam seemed to rise from the springy ground, bringing a dampness to Ellen's temples and beading her short upper lip.

"Sister Sarah was saying to Mama last night that the damp air of the bottoms is unhealthy," she told Chris.

"I've heard the men talking. They're worried about cholera."

They had reached the shade of a cottonwood tree where the ground was drier and they put the black willow limb down and rested, wiping perspiration from their foreheads and under their eyes. After a few minutes Chris took out his hatchet and began trimming. Ellen sat on the ground with her feet tucked under her long skirt, and watched him.

"What you making, boy?" a teamster walking by with a pail of water called.

"Yoke."

"That's a yoke?" The man laughed.

Chris chopped doggedly, ignoring him. He strolled back to camp and presently a couple of other men wandered out to the cottonwood tree, followed by a ragtail of children.

"What you gonna hitch with that yoke, Chris?" one of them called. "A sea serpent?"

"You'll see." He took out his knife and began whittling. In his concentration, his yellow locks fell over his forehead and he pushed his tongue out of the corner of his mouth.

All afternoon he labored on the strange, unequal yoke. Ellen watched, now and then fetching him a cool dipper of water. When it was peeled smooth they yoked Daisy and Buff, and Ellen ran to get Brother Safford.

The big, black-bearded man came silently, and silently ran his hand over the hump of wood that fitted Buff's big neck and sloped down to lie lightly across Daisy's. "Does it drive?"

Chris and Ellen looked at each other with quickening excitement. Chris ran to pick up the line, shouting, "Hi-i-*eeek!*"

Ellen found herself whispering, "Gently, Daisy,

very gently!" Then she laughed a catchy laugh as the two animals moved together. For once they pulled in unison, Daisy stepping lightly and quickly beside the ox's steady walk.

"It might work," the big man admitted, as Chris turned the team in a tight circle, and Ellen let out her breath in a long sigh.

Her mother helped her unyoke. "Did you know Brother Safford has been chosen leader of the train? I don't know what we would have done without him!"

"Or Chris," Ellen replied, her heart full.

She was to echo that thought again and again in the next days. If it had not been for Chris and his patient coaching she would never have learned to make the slow, stubborn animals obey her command.

By each nightfall she was almost in despair. Then with daylight came a cheery whistle outside the wagon, and Ellen slipped into her dusty clothes and joined the tall, yellow-haired boy waiting for her in the warm hush of the July morning for another day of practice on the broad trampled plain that had been used for the same purpose by each camp before them.

Each day they thought the next morning would see them on the road. Each night new cholera cases were reported at the meeting around the campfire, and prayers said for the recovery of the sick. Harriet Barlow's gentle hands were kept busy with her smelly black remedy.

"Misery Bottom," they named the campground, in wry humor, telling each other, "The disease is in the river fogs. We'll never be quit of it until we move on."

At last Brother Safford announced those unable to travel must be left behind. On a hot July morning the wagons of Ellen's company began moving out along the road plainly marked by those who had gone before them.

Women and girls walked beside their wagons. Older boys who did not have a yoke of oxen to drive were on horseback, herding the loose stock—milk cows, extra horses and oxen that belonged to the church. Joey followed Bertie Priddy and other children behind a band of sheep, a few goats and some pigs, with willow switches and yipping dogs to help keep them on the trail.

When Ellen took her place in the line of wagons, lantern and wash-pot and cookpots all dangling and jangling, she heard someone yelp, "Here comes the gypsy wagon!"

Men and women turned to smile, and the children took up the chant, "Look at the gypsies. We got gypsies!"

Ellen walked beside Daisy and Buff with her lead rope in one hand and a goad in the other, holding her bonneted head high.

"Haw!" she shouted. "Haw, Daisy! Buff!" The oxen strained against the crude humped yoke.

Let them laugh! She was on her way!

CHAPTER 10

THE canvas covers of the high stately Conestogas dipped and swayed along the rough trail, like the sails of sea-going schooners riding the waves. Some were drawn by two yokes of oxen, some by three. They stretched out in a long line that turned and twisted and coiled back on itself like a giant caterpillar.

Somewhere near its middle a girl walked beside a little green wagon drawn by a single yoke and hung from front to back with jangling utensils.

Clouds of dust hugged the train, and flies and other insects hovered over it. The rattle of the wheels and the creak of the wagons, the shouts of teamsters, barking dogs and bawling oxen mingled in a continuous roar of sound. Ellen's lips were soon dry and caked with dust, her hands blistered from the lead rope and burned by the sun.

They had been on the trail two weeks, climbing

76

hills, braking down steep dugways, wading through marshes and shallow streams. When Ellen drove her wagon up to take her place in camp that evening, she found herself next to the Safford wagons. By the time she unyoked, her mother and Joey were already at the Safford campfire and Sister Eliza called over to ask her to join them for supper.

Zina, her face hot and her eyes red from the smoke, was cooking skillet bread beside an iron pot of bubbling beans, while Diantha got out plates and forks from a box at the end of the wagonbed. Both girls looked hot, sunburned and tired. Ellen found a secret satisfaction in seeing that the Safford girls, too, were beginning to show the dust of the road.

"Zina put the beans to soak this morning," Sister Eliza was telling Ellen's mother in her soft voice. "I mixed the bread in the wagon and had it rising so it would be ready to fry."

"Here's fresh butter for it," Harriet Barlow said, with a touch of pride in her laughter, "churned by Daisy and Buff." She held up her teakettle. The spout was corked and a fresh cloth lay under the lid. "I hung Daisy's milk under the wagon this morning. With the jolting she and Buff gave it today, I couldn't have anything but butter!"

Never had food tasted better, but when she had eaten, Ellen's eyes were so heavy she wondered if she could keep them open long enough to find her way to their own wagon. She picked up her plate and took it over to the wagon projection where the Safford girls were preparing to wash dishes.

"You've done your day's work, Ellen," Sister Eliza exclaimed, taking her plate from her.

Ellen saw something dark and hostile flicker in Zina's eyes, but she did not care. She had done a day's work and she felt it in all her bones. She flung herself on the ground, as Chris and the other teamsters had done, and for a few moments it felt as soft as any feather bed.

Presently she noticed the boys were stealing out of the camp. "Where's everybody going?" she asked Chris, when he got to his feet.

"Down to the river to bathe, I reckon," he said, with a grin.

"Why don't you go with them, Ellen?" Zina mocked her, the outer corners of her eyes slanting upward.

"Oh, Zina, stop it!" Diantha said, but indifferently.

Ellen ignored them, but there was an angry tightness in her throat. *I hope I don't have to put up with her all the way to the Valley,* she told herself.

But it began to look as if she would. Ellen was baffled by the change in her mother. Harriet Barlow was one of the few women in the wagon train who seemed to grow stronger as they marched beside their wagons. Color had come back to her cheeks and life had returned to her eyes.

It was good to hear her laugh again. But her intense interest in the Safford family was disturbing, and her mother's praise of the bearded leader was beginning to get on Ellen's nerves. One morning she told her mother, pointedly, "We could not have begun our journey without Chris."

"Chris is a good boy," her mother agreed. She added, after a moment, "It was thoughtful of Brother Phineas to send him to help us," and Ellen exploded, "Oh, *Mama!*"

After a moment her mother said, as usual, "I think I'll just walk ahead to Sister Eliza's wagon and see if I can do anything to make her more comfortable."

Ellen looked after her, feeling an odd loneliness.

As she walked to the music of her creaking wheels, Ellen thought about Chris. They were in strange Indian territory now, and the men and older boys split the nights on guard duty. It was not easy for them to stay awake half the night, after driving oxen from daylight to dark.

Ellen had noticed Chris was growing thinner. Last night with the firelight silhouetting them, she had been shocked by the sharpness of his elbows, sticking out of the ragged sleeves of his shirt.

And that shirt! By the time they reached the high mountain valleys there would be nothing left of it, and cold weather would be on them. She knew he had no other.

The only solution she could see was not an easy one. She needed her linsey-woolsey skirt badly, but it was the only warm piece of material she or her mother could spare that was large enough to make a man's shirt.

She decided Chris needed it more than she did. She

would ask her mother to help her cut it. She could sew it evenings by the firelight, and if she started right away she could have it done by the time cold weather came. The decision filled her with a pleasant warmth that stayed with her through the day.

That night she was wakened from a sound sleep by a shouting and commotion.

"Whoa, there, you stubborn beasts! Whoa, *whoa, bally!*" The shouting was lost in the loud bawling of oxen and the terrifying sound of hooves thudding against hard ground.

"*Indians!*" The shrieks came from the darkness all about them. Ellen stuck her head out of the wagon but though the noise was like thunder and the wagon rocked as in an earthquake she could make out nothing in the darkness but great swirling clouds of dust.

"Indians! Lord help us!" screamed the women, but now men were shouting, "Stampede!"

Chris appeared out of the darkness. "There's no Indians," he said, and there was still enough light from the campfire to see his wide grin. "Tom Bedford had a nightmare—thought he was still driving team. He's scared the oxen into stampeding."

Hastily dressed men stood around the dying embers of campfires, some laughing and some out-of-sorts, wondering aloud whether they should go after the stock now or wait until daylight. A few went out but soon returned, saying the search was useless now. Gradually they straggled back to bed and the camp settled down to sleep once more.

At breakfast next morning they learned the train would be delayed at least a day while all the animals were rounded up. Harriet Barlow and her friends openly rejoiced at the opportunity to wash and iron and bake, and clean out their wagons.

At the meeting around the big campfire that night, the teamsters were told to hobble and tie their teams together from now on. The leaders of the train spoke with reproof in their voices about the day's delay, warning them three months' journeying lay ahead of them and they might expect snow in the mountains.

The brother who closed the meeting with prayer asked eloquently for the safety of the train from all dangers that might beset it, and when he finished a sober silence held around the fire.

Then from a group of young teamsters standing together came a high, squeaky voice saying, "Whoa, whoa, bally!" Everyone laughed. The children took up the shout, running about and mocking shrilly, "Whoa, bally! Whoa, bally!"

Young Tom Bedford shifted his feet, darted a quick glance at Diantha Safford, then dropped his eyes to gaze red-faced and tongue-tied into the fire.

Diantha turned on the laughing children. "Now, you quit it!" she scolded, color staining her smooth cheeks. "Do you want to stampede the cattle again?"

"Looks like the cattle ain't all he's stampedin'!" a boy called, and shouts of laughter went up again.

Ellen joined in the laughter until she happened to

meet Zina Safford's eyes. They were pools of anguished fury, and Ellen stared in surprise.

A moment later she wondered if she could have imagined it, as Zina tossed her dark head and laughed.

The next morning the train was underway again. They had left the winding hilly roads behind them when they left the Elk Horn, and were crossing a flat level country, with few trees. Often they traveled two wagons abreast to avoid each other's dust. There was plenty of room for those who were impatient to pass by the slower wagons.

Ellen was hard put to keep up, in spite of the lightness of her wagon. She was always with the wagons who straggled into camp at dark, with the dogs barking and the men and women around the fires saying, "It's only the Robbins and the Priddys and Sister Harriet's little gypsy."

She looked like a gypsy, her hands brown as a nutmeg, her face darkening in spite of the sunbonnet she wore. As she trudged along in the choking dust, her head ringing with the creaking of the axles and the mournful complaints of the oxen, Ellen dreamed of slipping out of her clothing and sliding into the cool cleansing waters of some secluded pool. But often she arrived in camp too late to go with the women to the creek to bathe.

One evening she determined to have her swim even if she must go alone. As usual, her mother was with Sister Eliza. The Safford girls had disappeared. Ellen slipped away from the camp and made her way to the creek.

She was trying to walk as quietly as an Indian, aware that she was doing a foolish and perhaps reckless thing. In her stealth she came upon a surprising sight down in the willows along the creekbed—two dark forms so close they almost merged, a murmur of voices like the cooing of the mourning dove.

Ellen stopped, her face flaming with embarrassment as she realized who the two she had intruded on were. Diantha Safford was old enough to have a beau, but— Tom Bedford! The shy and awkward teamster, teased by everyone because he cried out in his sleep at night, was a surprising choice for pretty, dainty Diantha!

Tom Bedford was not so shy now, Ellen thought, bending all her efforts toward backtracking quietly so the two should not discover her. When she was far enough from the clump of willows concealing them, she picked up her skirts to run.

Suddenly a shape before her she had thought was a bush took human form. The moon moved from behind a cloud and she recognized Zina, crouched over as if in pain, the traces of tears on her face.

There was such woe in her attitude that Ellen knew the other girl at this moment felt as lonely as she did and in a flash of understanding knew why. The two sisters had been very close. Now Diantha had a beau, and Zina could not go with her to meet him in the shadow of the willows.

Zina saw her and jumped to her feet. "You were spying on them!" she accused, in a tense harsh whisper. "You little *sneak!*"

Before she could stop herself, Ellen had slapped the other girl across the mouth.

Then she was running, running as fast as she could toward camp, while tears of rage and shame gathered in her eyes.

CHAPTER 11

THERE was talk of Indians in the conversations around the cooking fires. They had passed the burned wickiups of two Indian villages since leaving the Missouri, evidence the tribes were at war. The women were nervous and the men watchful.

"Remember we are friendly," Brother Safford cautioned in his talk before evening prayers.

The next day they forded Upper Loup Creek. Horsemen rode ahead of them into the river, testing its depth. The river was wide, the sandbar dividing it under water. Directly across from them the bank was too steep for the wagons. It was necessary to cross to the submerged sandbar and travel down it a half mile to a spot where the oxen could safely climb the opposite bank.

The sandbar proved to be full of treacherous holes. The Safford wagon slipped into one and Sister Eliza was badly shaken, but Ellen's little wagon made the trip easily. There were some advantages to having a light wagon!

Later, as they were traveling along the main Platte some two miles north of the river bed, a cloud of dust appeared down the trail ahead of them. It approached rapidly. Dark shapes emerged and became figures on horseback. The sound of pounding hooves came to them and with it the cry echoing down the train: "*Indians!*"

Women yelled at the children, their terrified shrieks mingling with the shouts and oaths of the teamsters as they hastily sought to form a circle with the wagons.

Ellen's mother had gone very pale. "Take Joey into the wagon with you. Keep him there," she said. "I've got to go to Sister Eliza."

"*Mama!*" Ellen's heart thudded in terror, but there was room for outrage, too. "Why don't you stay with your own family?" she cried, angrily.

"Shush! Do as I tell you!" Her mother picked up her skirts and ran.

Ellen spied Joey with some other young boys switching some squealing pigs to urge them under the wagons and into the circle. A man spoke sharply to them and they ran to their wagons, leaving the dogs to herd the pigs.

Joey clambered up with Ellen and they peered through the wagon cover as the half-naked savages galloped up. They drew their ponies up in a long line facing the mounted leaders of the train, who awaited them sitting calm and erect on their own horses.

A brief parley took place. Then several of the brethren wheeled and rode around the wagons, calling, "The Indians are peaceful. They want tobacco and sugar."

There was little tobacco in camp, Ellen knew. The Word of Wisdom forbade it to the Saints. She found the sack of sugar and with shaking hands tied a pouch from a square of factory and measured a precious cupful into it.

Presently the order came to move again. The Indians had spread their blankets along the trail, squatting impassive and dark behind them. As they drove their wagons past, the Saints dropped their gifts on the blankets. Ellen walked stiffly, her head lowered so her bonnet would hide her face. Joey watched through the back canvas flap, his eyes wide and scared.

As the little wagon passed, with a clink-clank of its dangling pots, a ripple of interest ran down the line of squatting dark figures. The Indians stared. Some called out, pointing at Ellen, the littlest teamster.

A grinning young brave leaped to his feet and swaggered along beside her. "Squaw?" he said, pointing to himself. The other Indians laughed.

With an effort Ellen kept her gaze straight ahead. She heard a horse pound up and slow to her team's pace. She scarcely dared raise her eyes.

Then she heard Brother Safford's firm voice. "Give me your line, Ellen, and climb in the wagon with Joey."

Gratefully, she obeyed. Crouching in the wagon with Joey and peering out at the dark, painted faces, she thought with anger of her mother leaving them to walk the length of those staring eyes alone.

Harriet Barlow did not return to her own wagon. When they camped for the night she sent Joey to tell Ellen to come to the Saffords' campfire for supper.

"Here comes the little squaw!" Charlie Safford greeted her, amid laughter.

"It wasn't funny!" Ellen protested, but she could laugh with them now.

Her mother fixed two plates and climbed with them into the wagon, saying Sister Eliza felt too tired to come down from her bed, and she would keep her company. The boys ate quickly and got out the horseshoes and began pitching a game. Brother Safford sat with his half-emptied plate on his knees staring somberly into the fire.

Joey, still keyed up, chattered about the Indians, and how many he could have killed if only he had had a gun, until Brother Safford reproved him.

"The Indian is our red cousin."

"And Ellen's beau," Zina mocked from the wagon extension where she and Diantha were washing dishes.

Ellen bent her head over her sewing to hide her anger. She could take teasing from anyone but Zina!

Presently Diantha came and sat at the fire, looking curiously at Ellen's work. "It's a man's shirt, isn't it? Who's it for?"

"It's a surprise," Ellen said, distantly.

Zina flung the dishwater into the darkness away from the wagon and joined them at the fire. When Chris walked up a few moments later to warm his hands, her gaze narrowed on the way his sharpened elbows stuck out of his torn shirt.

She climbed into her mother's wagon and returned in a moment with a hickory shirt. "Hyrum's grown too big for this, Chris. Mother wants to know if you wouldn't like to have it."

His eyes lit up with pleasure as he thanked her. Ellen forced herself to sew calmly, hoping no one guessed her disappointment. Glad as she was for Chris, she felt sure Zina had been trying to belittle her gift of the linsey-woolsey shirt.

She waited only a few minutes then left the fire and went to her little wagon. She undressed and crawled under her buffalo robe on the provision chest, but she could not go to sleep.

Her heart was hard against Zina Safford, but it was hard against her mother, too. Why must they spend so much time with the Saffords? Couldn't her mother see how things were between her and Zina? It seemed to her that since they had begun their journey her mother had more time to give to Sister Eliza's family than to her own!

Sometime in the night she was wakened by low voices outside her wagon. The glare from a lantern penetrated her canvas cover. She parted it and looked outside.

Brother Safford carried the lantern. He was looking

down at her mother, who had pulled her dress on hastily and whose hair still hung in two fat braids across her shoulders.

"—I am afraid she is going," she heard Brother Safford say, with a note in his deep voice that made Ellen shiver.

She drew in her breath sharply. They both turned and looked up at her and her shock deepened when she saw her mother's eyes swimming in tears.

"It's Sister Eliza. Her heart is failing," Harriet told Ellen. She put her hand on Brother Phineas' arm. "Come, we must go to her."

Ellen looked after them in silence. She understood now why her mother had been so concerned about Sister Eliza, and felt a deep shame for her blindness.

At the same time the sight of her mother's hand resting lightly on Brother Safford's arm brought a rush of emotion that was close to panic.

CHAPTER 12

E VEN Sorrow must eat," Ellen's mother told her the
next evening, as she prepared a big supper.

The Safford wagons straggled in after dark. They
had stayed to heap rocks on the spot where they had
buried Sister Eliza. Because of the lateness of the
season, Brother Safford had insisted the rest of the
train move on after prayers were said at his wife's
grave.

The Safford men's faces showed their gratitude for
the hot food ready for them when they had finished
taking care of their stock, but Zina and Diantha sat in
frozen grief, leaving their plates almost untouched. In
spite of their differences, Ellen found her heart wrung
with pity for them.

From that night on, Harriet Barlow prepared meals
for the two families together.

The appearance of the country through which they

traveled had changed. They were skirting sandy bluffs at the foot of which ran water from cool springs. A few willows grew along the streams but the high ground was barren. Only prickly pears grew there, and wild sage which gave off a pungent odor as the wagon wheels crushed it.

It was increasingly difficult to find wood for campfires. As soon as the company stopped, Joey and Bertie and their friends were sent to gather buffalo chips, which were numerous and made quite a satisfactory fire.

One evening as Ellen approached the campfire after caring for her team, she heard Diantha telling Zina in a low, bitter voice, "That's the trouble with a wagon train—there's no privacy in it."

Ellen's temper flared. "I didn't ask to sit at your campfire! I don't like it any better than you do."

Diantha said, in a startled tone, "But I didn't mean—"

Ellen's mother turned from the wagon extension where she was beating biscuits. "Ellen! Shame on you, talking that way!"

"Ellen." A dark shape loomed beyond the fire. It was Brother Safford, his deep voice sorrowful, yet stern. "I want you to hear what I am going to tell the girls. Diantha, Zina—you know that Sister Harriet was with your mother the night she passed away. Her last words were, 'Sister Harriet, take care of my family.' And Sister Harriet made a promise to her—and to me."

Ellen met Zina's dark eyes. They seemed to reflect

her own dismay. She choked, "*I* didn't make any promises!" and turned and ran for the privacy of the little wagon.

She climbed up over the wheel and crawled in to throw herself on her hard bed. Lying there in the dark with the now-familiar sounds of camp around her—the dogs barking, someone chopping sagebrush, the clink-clank of a belled and hobbled ox and the twang of a fiddle from a distant campfire—it seemed as if she had lived this way forever. Tonight she longed to be free of it. Oh, to have a house roof over her once again! To crawl between the sheets of a real bed, to hear her father moving through the rooms in the early morning making the fires.

"Ellen?" It was her mother's voice, just outside the wagon.

She did not reply, and Harriet climbed in. She set down a plate of hot food and lit the lantern. In its light her face looked troubled.

"Ellen, I must tell you something you may have guessed."

Ellen's heart began a complicated rhythm, so loud she wondered if her mother heard it.

"You heard Brother Safford. You know, don't you, what he was trying to tell you?"

Ellen did not answer.

"When we reach the Valley, we will be—he has asked me to—be his wife."

She could see how hard it was for her mother to say those words. She said, faintly, "Mama, *no*—" trying to

control the boiling up within her that was almost
nausea.

"I've been hoping you and Zina and Diantha would
come to understand each other better."

She'd been hoping— Ellen said, in shock, "How long
have you planned this?"

"Sister Eliza spoke of it many times. I think we all
knew she could not survive the trip. She was worried
about leaving her family."

"You might have asked how I felt about it!" Ellen
burst out, violently.

"You and Joey need a father. A woman alone in a
pioneer country—"

"We don't need the Saffords! Haven't we got along
without Papa for two years? We can do it, Mama. I
know we can!"

Harriet Barlow reached out to smooth her daughter's hair. "Pray about it, Ellen. Ask the Lord to help
you accept it."

Ellen jerked away and buried her face in her arms.
Her mother left the plate of food behind her, but Ellen
could not eat.

All the next day she watched Brother Safford closely,
a hard coldness in her stomach. Sitting his bay mare
authoritatively, he rode up and down the train, bel-
lowing orders from his deep chest—and between them
Ellen saw another shadowy figure, thin and wiry, with
laughter in his eyes and a soft brown beard that tickled
her face. *I won't forget you, Papa,* she said, in her
heart.

Brother Safford seemed to have put his grief behind him. After the stock had been taken care of and the campfire built that evening, he walked out in the circle formed by the wagons with a handful of horseshoes, shouting a challenge. Soon the sharp clang of iron shoes on the hard ground reverberated through the camp.

"Give Zina a hand with dinner tonight, Ellen," her mother said, in a firm, no-nonsense voice. "Sister Stewart's baby is feverish and she has asked me to look in on him."

Ellen moved toward the fire where Zina was stirring some meal into hot water. A cold look passed between the girls. Some pieces of sidemeat were beginning to warm in a skillet and Ellen picked up a long fork to turn them. The silence grew hurting.

Presently Ellen said, "Where's Diantha?"

"Gone off with Tom Bedford to look for wood." Zina gave a derisive snort. "Wood—in this desert!"

Ellen wondered if Zina had understood what her father was telling them last night. "If she doesn't know, she won't hear it from me," she thought.

She almost jumped when Zina said, in a hard defensive voice, "They're going to be married. They've asked Papa to perform the ceremony," she went on, and Ellen realized she was still talking about her sister and Tom Bedford.

"I should think they'd wait until we reach the Valley," Ellen ventured.

"They're sentimental about it. They fell in love on

the plains and they want to be married on the plains."

"I see." Ellen bent over the fire. "It—is romantic, isn't it?"

"It's sickening!" Zina burst out. "I'm sick of the whole thing!"

"Tom seems nice," Ellen said, defensively.

"Oh, for heaven's sake!" Zina looked at her with contempt, and Ellen felt the unsteady rage push up toward her throat. She could never be sister to this girl!

After supper she walked away from camp toward the willows on the creek where she had left her team. She recognized Daisy's bell and its familiarity was comforting. A yellow September moon hung above the bluff on the horizon, lighting her way.

Daisy lowed a greeting. She put her arms around the cow's neck, her loneliness somewhat relieved by the animal warmth she could feel through her dress and by the relaxed rhythm of Daisy's chewing.

A sound startled her. Someone was moving in the willows. "Who's there?" she called. A tall form stepped out of the darkness. "Chris?"

"I saw you leave the fire. I didn't think you should go so far from camp alone." He gave her a sharp look. "Something's bothering you, isn't it?"

"Yes." He might as well know. "Mama and Brother Safford are going to be married when we get to the Valley."

Chris nodded. "I figured so."

Maybe everyone in camp had seen it coming but

herself. Hadn't she guessed, too, but not wanted to admit it? A lump rose in her throat. "Am I supposed to be happy about it? Well, I'm not!"

Chris had squatted and was stripping some sage-brush. "Notice how much colder it's getting? We're climbing, even if it don't look like it." He lit the brush and they warmed their hands over the small flame. She was a little ashamed of her outburst and grateful that he ignored it.

"Fort Laramie's only a day or two away. Some of the men are going over to see if they can buy more supplies there. But only those appointed can go." A strange half-bitter tone crept into his voice. "They're afraid to mix with the gold-seekers goin' through on the other side of the river."

"There's lots of Missourians seeking gold."

"Yes," he said, in an odd voice. After a moment he added, "I wouldn't tell anybody else—I'm going to the Fort if I have to sneak over at night."

"Your father?" Ellen guessed.

"Somebody might have seen him." Chris put some more sage strippings on the fire and the acrid smoke rose between them. His long face was tanned by the weeks of sun and out of it his eyes looked startlingly blue.

"This is new country you're going to. I wonder if you know how different it will be?"

"How can it be so different from Kanesville? That was a wilderness until Papa and the other men felled trees and put up cabins and dugouts."

"Who will put up your cabin in the Valley?" Chris asked her, and she realized with irritation that he had trapped her. "Joey needs a father. Have you noticed how he has steadied under the discipline of the journey? It's been good for him. You and Joey and your mother need Phineas Safford."

His use of Brother Safford's full name struck her ear oddly. It was the first time in weeks she had realized that Chris was not one of them.

She stirred uneasily, stretching her hands across the small fire. "We don't need him as much as Mama thinks we do," she said, voicing the resentment that had been growing in her ever since the journey began. "She even thanked him for sending you to help us!"

Chris laughed.

"The Lord and Brother Safford have done it all!"

"If you're trying to give credit, Ellen, it's all of us working together that's going to get us to the Valley."

"Oh, that isn't what's bothering me!" she cried, impatiently. "If you want to know the truth, Chris, it's Zina. How can I stand to live in the same house with her?"

His laughter pealed like a bell on the crisp air.

Ellen stared at him half angrily, knitting her brows. "What's so funny?"

"Why, you and Zina are as like as two peas!"

"Chris!" Outrage completely filled her.

"I'm sorry," he said, but she didn't believe him at all. He still looked as if he were laughing.

"I thought you were *my* friend," she said, angrily, and turned away.

"Listen, Ellen—" He grabbed her arm.

"Oh, leave me alone!" she cried, shaking off his hand. She ran toward camp, the salty taste of pain in her mouth. Yet even in her anguish, she was reminded of Zina, crouched in woe the night she stumbled on her in the darkness near where Tom was making love to Diantha.

Were they alike? No—no—never! She hated Zina Safford!

CHAPTER 13

THE next day Diantha walked openly beside Tom
Bedford as he drove his team, and Zina walked
alone. The two sisters scarcely spoke to each other
when they made camp that evening.

Ellen told herself, "It's no skin off my nose!" But
she could not help wondering if they had quarreled
over Diantha's romance.

The road continued along the foot of the bluffs,
passing strange rock formations.

"Look! A castle!" Bertie Priddy cried.

Joey pointed. "That one's a chimney."

"That must be Chimney Rock!" a man exclaimed.

"Haun's Mill," a woman said, softly, and a chill
passed over all who heard. At Haun's Mill their cabins
had been burned by the mob, leaving only a handful
of tall, blackened chimneys standing.

Talk of Missourians ran from wagon to wagon as the

painful memories were recalled. Many were apprehensive of meeting old enemies at Fort Laramie, where the road along the north bank of the Platte, used by the Mormon trains, would merge with the road of the gold-seekers, who had been traveling the south bank.

Brother Safford rode from wagon to wagon advising the Saints that they would camp on the river as soon as they had forded Laramie Fork. He ordered all to stay in camp while he and the captains went to the fort to inquire if they could buy food supplies, for some families were running low.

While the wagons were fording the stream, a group of horsemen rode out from the adobe walls of the fort to meet the company. They galloped up to Brother Safford, who sat on his horse directing the fording.

Ellen stuck her head around her little wagon to stare at the rough-looking men in their buckskin clothing, and wrinkled her nose. They smelled just like the Indians who used to stand around Brother Atkins' stove back in Kanesville.

"Have your people any surplus supplies they would sell?" she heard one ask, after greetings had been exchanged.

" 'Twould lighten your wagons for the mountain passes," his companion added, curbing his impatient horse.

"I see the California emigrants have been ahead of us," Brother Safford observed, wryly. "We had hoped to buy foodstuffs from you."

"We can't get enough for all who want to buy."

"I'm sorry I can't help you, gentlemen. Can you give us information about the mountain passes?"

"You're risking snow this time of year. Better push on fast as you can."

"There are men over at the fort who just came in from the Salt Lake Valley," a second man said. "Why not ride over and talk with them yourself?"

"A good idea." Brother Safford placed Brother Stewart in charge of the fording and, calling the captains to accompany him, rode away with his visitors.

Ellen could scarce get her team unyoked for staring about her. After the long lonely weeks on the untraveled road north of the Platte, this was civilization of a rough sort. The river was lined with wagons, and women were doing their wash or baking bread over their campfires. A girl sat on a wagon tongue drying her hair in the sun—it fanned over her shoulders and fell to her hips like a golden shawl.

Not far away were the tanned hide wickiups of an Indian camp and a corral of ponies the red men had brought to sell to the travelers. A squaw with a papoose on her back trudged toward the fort.

Closer to the fort was a cluster of army tents and around the fort itself was ranged every kind of equipage for crossing the plains, from packs of laden mules to buggies, yankee wagons and the big "prairie schooners."

A pack train of fur trappers with an Indian guide passed by the Mormon wagons, looking them over curiously. As Ellen stared back, a rough-looking man with hair curling to his shoulders spat disgustedly.

"The mountains will be as crowded as the streets of St. Louis if they keep comin'!" she heard him say.

She finished with her team and walked down to the water's edge in a secluded spot to wash the dust of the day's journey from her face and hands. As she started back to her wagon, she saw a lone figure emerge from the low brush near camp and walk in the direction of the fort.

It was Chris. He really was going to visit the fort by himself, deliberately disobeying Brother Safford! But, of course, he was not *Brother* Safford to Chris.

She and her mother and Joey spent the next day cleaning the wagon, scrubbing clothes and mending the equipment, preparing for the hardest part of the journey which lay ahead of them in the high mountains.

"Will your cart hold together till we reach the Valley?" Brother Priddy asked Ellen, bluntly.

The wheels were loose on the axle and they leaned in, giving the little wagon a spraddled look. The fresh green paint Chris had brushed on was sun-faded and grayed with dust now, and the canvas had blackened over the bows from the thundershowers.

"It's still a sturdy wagon," Ellen claimed, stoutly. By this time it was almost as dear to her as were Daisy and Buff. The beasts showed the mark of travel, too. Both were so thin their ribs showed under their matted hides. Ellen was glad they were having a day of rest.

That evening was different from all other evenings on the trail. When dusk fell the sound of loud laughter and raucous singing to a lively fiddle carried clearly over the desert to the Mormon camp.

After the Saints finished their evening meal they gathered around a huge bonfire. Brother Safford proposed that two men be given horses and sent ahead, traveling rapidly, to ask that Saints in the Valley send out provision wagons and extra stock to meet them in the mountains.

Someone started a hymn, and soon the sounds of revelry from Fort Laramie were drowned by a mighty chorus of voices—men's, women's and children's—singing in unison:

> *"Come, come, ye Saints,*
> *No toil nor labor fear.*
> *But with joy wend your way!"*

A prayer was said. Then a brother brought out his fiddle. The stars were thicker than mosquitoes in the dark sky and the air was sharp with burning sage as they danced to the happy rhythm of the *Arkansas Traveler*.

Ellen danced with Hyrum Safford, who reminded her of a big awkward bear. When a new reel formed, Charlie was waiting to claim her. Younger than Hyrum and unsure of himself, he was still much lighter on his feet. Flushed and happy, Ellen looked about for Chris but could not find him in the throng around the fire.

Long after the Saints had closed their evening's

relaxation with another prayer and retired to their wagons, the loud voices and snatches of music from the fort came to their ears, buffeted and torn by a rising wind. Ellen lay awake for a long time, wondering if Chris were among the roistering men. She hadn't seen him since he headed for the fort the evening before.

Suppose he didn't come back? Suppose he had found someone going on to the gold fields who needed an extra teamster?

No, she told herself, Chris had made an agreement with Brother Safford, and he knew the Mormon leader needed him. But she tossed and turned, sorry she had lost her temper the last time she and Chris talked. She needed him, too. She could never have come so far without his help and encouragement.

The next morning the train moved on, their trail joining the trail of the gold-seekers who had been traveling the south bank of the Platte. The Oregon emigrants had come this way, and before them the fur trappers, and before them the Indians.

Chris galloped up to the little Barlow wagon on an Indian pony Brother Safford had bought at the fort. His brown face was split in a wide grin.

"You've had some news?"

"How did you know?"

She tossed her head. "Daisy told me."

"She's a witch." Chris laughed, a joyous laugh. "Ellen, I've found my father! At least, I've found where he was last spring. He was at a place called Hangtown, in the gold-rush country."

"Oh, Chris, I'm so glad for you!"

"Yuppeeee!" With a wild Indian yell he slapped his pony and galloped back to the Safford wagons, singing at the top of his voice. Heads turned as he passed, and faces hardened. He was singing one of the songs that had floated across from the fort the night before.

They had left the river and for eighty miles found their camping spots beside creeks or springs, some with surprising warm water. When they came again to the Platte, at the North Fork, they found two rough-looking men operating a ferry made from hewn logs. They had been sent by Brigham Young to provide a river crossing for the wagon trains.

"Carry fresh water," the ferrymen told them. "Don't delay, or winter will catch you in the mountains. Whatever you do, don't camp by an alkali spring. You'll lose your stock if they drink from it."

The next day they left the river for the last time. Each morning Ellen and her mother had been filling a wooden tub with cold water in which they carried their butter and milk. This time they filled it with extra drinking water.

The countryside through which they traveled now, between the Platte and the Sweetwater, was a strange and menacing one, marked by singular rocks and a profusion of mineral springs and lakes. The lakes were ringed with white saleratus. Ellen's mother filled a sack with it and hung it from a wagon bow. When they made camp she grated it in her spice mill, put it in water and let it settle, then used the solution for leavening hot biscuits for supper.

They were round and high and lightly browned on top, and they disappeared into Brother Safford's black beard with amazing rapidity. Finally, he wiped his lips with the back of his hand and sighed, "Sister Harriet, those are the best biscuits I've ever eaten."

"Mmmm," mumbled Hyrum through a full mouth. He was growing both tall and broad, like his father in all ways except that the beard he was beginning to sprout looked as if it would be red.

Charlie would never be as big, but he was very like a beardless, more compact Phineas Safford. He snatched up another biscuit, frankly greedy.

Across the fire Zina dropped her plate and leaped to her feet. Her eyes, hot and accusing, were on them both. "Mama made better biscuits than this, and you know it!"

A little hush fell over the two-family group, touching even Joey, whose eyes widened on Zina. Diantha looked down at the dusty shoes sticking out from the edge of her skirt and reached for Tom's hand.

Ellen thought, "So they know." For the first time she noticed that Zina's eyes were red-rimmed, as if from weeping.

"Zina," her father said, sternly, "apologize to Sister Harriet!"

"What for?" Zina demanded, tears glittering on her dark lashes. "It was the truth. I can't stand the way you're all fawning over her!"

"Zina!" His voice was a bellow of rage.

The girl turned and ran into the darkness.

Ellen's mother was pale, but her voice was steady as she picked up the big stirring spoon from the pot on the fire and asked, "Would anyone like some more beans?"

Later that night, after Ellen had crawled in under her buffalo robe, she heard the oxen bawling as if disturbed, and the clink of their hobbles as they tried to run. She got out of her bed, shivering, and poked her head between the canvas flaps of the wagon.

The sounds had ceased and the night was still and starry and very cold. Nothing stirred. Just as she pulled her head back a shadow moved, running, across the space between two wagons. It was Zina. What was she doing among the stock?

Ellen recalled her red-rimmed eyes and wondered uneasily if Zina had been out alone with her heartache all this time.

"There's no privacy in a wagon train," Diantha had complained, and it was true. Not even for weeping. Shivering, Ellen crept back in bed.

In the morning when she went out to yoke her team, Buff was missing.

CHAPTER 14

CHARLIE SAFFORD and Chris mounted the Indian pony, one behind the other, and rode out to look for Ellen's ox. The rest of the company pushed on, and Brother Safford sent his wagons with them.

"Whyn't they abandon that gypsy cart?" a passing man grumbled. "It'll never hold up in the mountains, anyway."

"Seems like Brother Safford could get all it holds in one of his wagons now," his wife replied.

Ellen pretended not to hear, but her meaning was clear. Already the Saints thought of the Barlows and the Saffords as one family.

She was puzzled about Buff's wandering off. She knew she had hobbled the ox securely, and a hobbled ox could not get out of sight in this country overnight.

A distant shot echoed above the familiar medley of shouts and dogs and creaking wagons. A few minutes later the two boys came galloping toward camp. Chris was waving something.

Brother Safford rode up as they dismounted. "We found him lyin' by a foul-smellin' water hole," Charlie told his father. "Couldn't get him up."

"Alkali poisoning," his father said, regretfully.

Chris handed Ellen the torn leather strap. "We had to shoot him," he said, his eyes sorry. "He was past helping. Looks like he cut his hobble on a rock, don't it?"

Ellen's eyes filled with tears. "Or somebody cut it for him."

"Now, Ellen, who would do a thing like that?" Brother Safford chided her.

Your daughter, she wanted to say. But she bit back the accusing words. She couldn't prove Zina was responsible.

"Cut out an ox from the church herd for Ellen, Charlie," his father told him. "Then start the herd moving. Chris, help her yoke."

It was a difficult, bitterly exhausting day, breaking in another ox to pull with Daisy in the humped yoke.

That night at supper Zina was flushed and talkative. Ellen was silent until Brother Safford asked, "Well, Ellen, how did you and the new ox get along?"

"He's strong, but not as smart as Buff." Ellen looked straight at Zina. "You wouldn't think an ox would know he could cut his hobble on a rock, would you?"

Zina glanced at her, then quickly away, but Ellen had seen a glitter of fear in her eyes. She felt a moment of triumph. Someday she would make Zina admit she had done it!

With each day they climbed higher and the sun was no longer warm. At night Ellen pulled the buffalo robes close around her. The climbing began to take a toll among the old. Nerves were frayed and limbs exhausted. Another wagon stopped for a brief burial beside the trail.

Sometimes they passed mounds of stones or a wooden marker left by those who had gone before—reminders of the grimness of their struggle.

Once they passed a grave that had been opened by wolves. It was a grisly sight, with rotted clothing and bones scattered about. The rough board marker had been tipped by the digging, but still legible were the words painted on it:

E. DODD

GALLATIN, MO.

D. 19 JULY 1848

OF TYPHUS FEVER.

"Why don't we bury the poor wretch again?" Chris suggested to the little group who had paused to read it.

There was a silence, then a woman's hard voice said, "A Missourian!"

"There was a Dodd with the murdering mob at Haun's Mill!"

An angry brother stepped close to Chris. "Maybe you want to bury your friend, boy, but don't ask the Saints to help you!"

"My friend?" Chris repeated, sounding surprised.

"What were you doing over at Fort Laramie when you were supposed to be tending your stock?"

"Maybe he's in the pay of the Missourians, spying on us!"

Chris looked bewildered as his eyes traveled from one stony face to another.

Shocked by the attack on him, Ellen pushed her way through the growing group around the open grave. Before she could reach his side she heard Zina's voice, crying, "For shame! Chris had good reason to go to the fort."

"He went to seek news of his father who's in the gold fields!" Ellen chimed in.

Brother Stewart said, good-naturedly, "The girls are sticking up for you, anyway, Chris," and there was scattered laughter, breaking the tension.

Brother Safford had ridden up on his big bay. "We've no time to waste on past quarrels. Let's move on, brethren!"

"Thanks for speaking up for me, Zina," Ellen heard Chris say, as she turned obediently back to her team.

She wondered who besides herself had seen Chris going to the fort. It troubled her to think that some of the Saints were suspicious of him.

Chris was troubled, too. He sat silent by the fire after his chores that evening, and went to bed right after supper.

Moving more and more slowly, the long train reached the Sweetwater, coming to the large mound of stone called Independence Rock, on which hundreds of travelers had inscribed their names and the date. The wagons stopped and the Saints swarmed over the rock, cutting their own names into its smooth surface and telling each other the end of a difficult journey was near.

They forded the Sweetwater and went on, with the roar of waters rushing through Devil's Gate coming to their ears. It was nearing the end of September. Overnight the skies changed from blue, with piled-up-icing clouds, to a dull leaden gray.

Brother Safford and his captains watched them anxiously, and *snow* was the thought in everyone's mind. Toward evening of the second of October, as they traveled a broad plain, a few white flakes swirled lazily down. In moments, a falling snow was silently curtaining the wagons.

It had come like a ghost and now it filled the air with feathery movement and a curiously disturbing stillness. It blunted sounds, muting their footsteps and the bawling of cattle. Even the creaking of the wagon wheels seemed deadened and without weight.

For an hour or more the company pushed on while the ground whitened. Though the climb had been imperceptible, they knew by the cold thin air that they were very high. When they reached a branch of the Sweetwater the order came back from the head of the train to make camp.

By the time they had formed the circle, the wagons on the other side were obscured in the falling snow and early darkness. Ellen's fingers were almost too stiff with cold to do her bidding when she began to unyoke. For the first time, fearful and uneasy, she heard the shrill keening noise that heralds a blizzard sweeping down the high mountain valleys from the whitened Rockies.

It was a distant roar at first, rising in tone and volume as it came near until it was shrill as the sound of a saw. But this was no puny man-made noise. This was the shrieking of a cold evil wind, mightier than man or beast and threatening both. It struck terror to the hearts of the travelers, standing beside the insignificant shelter of their wagons.

In a matter of minutes it struck, overturning one wagon broadside to it and lifting off several wagon covers. The men worked fast, righting the overturned wagon and chaining the wagons together in their circle. Ellen clung to her oxbow, turning her back to the stinging snow driven on the wind. Her wagon rocked but stood up.

Chris appeared out of the white darkness. "Climb into the wagon with your mother and Joey," he shouted in her ear. "I'll finish unyoking."

"Where will they go?" Ellen cried, pitying the poor beasts.

He gestured toward the willows on the creek. "They'll find some shelter there. It's the best we can do. They won't wander off in this."

Joey came struggling against the wind with something buttoned beneath his coat, making it bulge mis-

shapenly in front. His mother reached to pull him to
the wagon. "What on earth is that?" she screamed
against the wind.

The little red dog that had been at Joey's heels as
he and Bertie herded the small stock poked his head
up and licked Joey under the chin.

"You can't bring him in the wagon," Harriet Barlow said, firmly.

Joey looked at her with eyes that were no longer a
child's. "If I don't, he'll die."

For a moment they faced each other. Then Harriet
made a resigned gesture that had something of fear
for them all in it. "Hurry, then," she said, and Ellen
helped Joey clamber up with his warm burden.

All night long, while the wind shrieked around the
wagon, they lay huddled together on the provisions
box that had been Ellen's and her mother's bed, their
bodies pressed close to keep each other warm. The dog
lay at their feet and Ellen was grateful for his warmth,
although his wet doggy smell, combined with the odor
of the tanned buffalo robes, was overpowering.

Outside the wind rose in high keening. The canvas
blew in against the wagon bows and the little wagon
rocked in sudden blasts. When the wind was strongest
they held the wagon cover on with their bare hands,
bracing the bows with their bodies, and when it calmed
enough to let go, their fingers and backs ached with
tension and cold.

When they were hungry Harriet rummaged in the

provisions for some of Ellen's rusk and they nibbled on that.

Morning came and the wind was still raging. Ellen lifted the canvas and looked out on a world bleached of all color. White blanketed the sagebrush and the low hills along the river. There was no line between hill and sky. The wind came screaming down from the northeast, blowing the powdery dry snow before it like cutting sand.

She could not see farther than the third wagon on each side. Two more had lost their covers, the curved ribs standing bare as bleached bones in the gray light. Each wagon was isolated, a dwelling to itself. No one ventured out into the stinging blizzard. They were cut off from their animals, and it would be folly to try to build a fire.

All day long the wind howled and shrieked around the little wagon. They heard no other sound, and they felt terribly alone. They continued to lie together for warmth and when they could sleep no longer Harriet began to sing. Ellen and Joey joined in, and when Red lifted his nose and began a companionable if melancholy howling, they laughed for the first time since the storm began.

In late afternoon a lull came in the storm. The wind still rocked the wagon, but gently, as if it were a cradle. Above its noise Ellen heard a faint sound at the end of the wagon and hurried to lift the cover. Chris stood there, looking comical with a woolen stocking pulled down over his ears.

"Are you all right in here?"

"Chris, come in out of the storm! You shouldn't be out in it," she scolded him, but her cheeks were warm with pleasure that he had come.

He climbed over the end of the wagon. His head almost brushed the cover, and it seemed both more crowded and warmer inside. He checked the cover fastenings and secured several that were loosened. The Saffords had lost covers from three of the four wagons in their charge, he told them. All of them, Tom Bedford and himself as well as the family, were huddled in the one still covered.

"Tom and Diantha are sitting as close as two kernels on a cob," he joked.

Ellen brought out the gray linsey shirt, finished at last. "You need this," she told him, shyly.

He took it with a look of pleasure, saying only, "I hoped it was for me."

He did not stay long, but his visit cheered them.

Later that evening Sister Priddy struggled over from the wagon next to them to peer in. "I just 'ad to come! I feel like I'm the only living thing in this desert." She had a cup of hot tea. "I'll give up my tea when I reach the Valley," she had said, when someone reminded her of the Word of Wisdom. "The Lord wouldn't ask it of me now!"

Harriet took the hot drink, marveling.

"I 'eated the water over my little fish-oil lamp. And it wasn't the first time. But it wasn't the easiest, either, in this wind." She laughed. "If I'd set my wagon on fire, there's some would have called it the Lord's punishment."

"God bless you," Harriet told her.

"It's medicine," she told her children sternly when their neighbor had struggled back to her own wagon. "Let it warm your stomachs and be thankful." She sweetened the hot and bitter drink and gave them rusk to dip in it, and that was their supper.

And still the wind keened around the wagon, drifting the snow in every direction.

CHAPTER 15

O N the second morning they awoke to a welcome
    stillness. Ellen struggled up from the smelly bed
to find the air bitterly cold. The sky overhead, when
she looked outside, was a brilliant blue and the white-
ness around them was dazzling. With snow drifted to
the wheeltops, the wagons seemed swimming in a
white sea. Down by the creek the willows drooped with
the weight of the snow, but even as she looked it began dropping off, letting the willow wands spring up
black and bare again.

Men were up, shoveling snow away from their wagons, clearing space for a campfire. Others waded
through the snow toward the willows, leaving narrow
trails behind them. There were few covers left intact
on the wagons. Heads raised from the wagon beds to
call anxious inquiries and offer reassurance.

Chris saw Ellen and waved. "Stay in until we get

some fires going. No use freezing your toes."

"How can we make a fire with no wood?" she wondered aloud.

Behind her Joey was scrambling out of the warm nest they had made under the tent cover, pulling on his heavy coat.

"Joey, the snow's too deep for you," Ellen protested.

He glanced at her briefly. "There's feeding to be done."

"Let him go," her mother said, quietly.

Ellen watched him as he took the shovel and began clearing snow away from a pen of geese hanging beneath a nearby wagon. Her brother was growing up.

The men were coming back from the willows in a discouraged file, following a trail they had broken through the snow. They stood in a little knot before the Safford wagons, talking in low tones. Joey laid his shovel down and went to stand with them.

Ellen and her mother watched anxiously. Presently the group broke and scattered. Brother Safford and Joey and Chris came wading through the deep snow with grave expressions.

"I knew it was too cold for those poor beasts," Ellen's mother said under her breath.

Both Joey and Chris were looking at Ellen and she knew at once what their somber eyes were telling her. "Daisy-Very-Gently?"

"Frozen," Joey said.

She could have wept for the little cow but for the knot of worry about their own fate.

"Our losses are serious," Brother Safford told her mother. "We counted nigh seventy animals frozen, half buried in the snow." He shook his head sadly and it hung so low his beard rested on his chest. "We must give thanks to God for sparing our own lives."

"We're not in the Valley yet!" Sister Priddy reminded him from the next wagon. Her sharp little nose was blue with cold, and a drop of moisture hung at its very tip.

"We have already sent ahead to the Valley for supplies," Brother Safford reminded her. "We will have to despatch another express with the news we are caught by a storm." He seemed to rouse himself and gather his strength. "First, we must have a fire and warm food for everyone. Please throw out anything you can discard that will burn. How are your supplies holding out, Sister Harriet and Sister Priddy?"

"We've not much left," the Englishwoman said.

"I can stretch ours two—maybe three weeks," Ellen's mother said slowly.

"It may not be enough." The bearded leader turned to his two daughters who were approaching, wrapped up like Indians in the quilts from their bed. "Diantha, Zina, I want to know how many pounds of flour and sugar and beans we have left."

"They're all getting low," Diantha told him.

"Check all our foodstuffs carefully and report to me."

Men were building a fire in a space cleared of snow, circled by the wagons. Nearly empty provisions boxes were emptied and chopped up. Someone threw in a chair, and Ellen and Joey dragged up the hump-backed yoke. They wouldn't need it now.

"Whyn't you throw on your wagon while you're at it?" Hyrum Safford called.

"Whyn't you burn your own?" Joey retorted, angrily.

"I still got a team."

Try as she might, Ellen could not get out of her mind the memory of Daisy-Very-Gently standing so still in the willows that early summer morning where she had hidden to escape her bewildering new burden. No more yoke for Daisy, she thought, sorrowing.

Would they really burn her little wagon now? It might come to that. They had to have fires to stay alive in this snow.

As the fire burned high, the women crept from their beds to warm themselves and to prepare the first hot meals in two days. The sun sparkled on the drifted snow, but it did not melt it. Nor did it warm the travelers half so much as the hot food.

After they had eaten, they held a meeting around the big campfire to discuss their plight. "We have two choices," Brother Safford told them. "We can lighten our loads, leave our freight here and go on with what oxen we have left, taking nothing but foodstuffs with us. Or, we can wait here for the supply wagons and extra stock Brother Brigham is sending out from the Valley."

"I move we wait here!" a man called. He was an English convert, with several wagonloads of household furnishings.

"Wait here!"

"I say we move on!"

"The beasts we have left cannot pull our wagons in this snow," another objected, "and it will be even harder in the mountains."

"We have a supply of meat here in our frozen stock that we can't haul."

"Those skinny old oxen?" a woman exclaimed.

"They could save our lives!"

"I haven't shipped my furniture across an ocean and hauled it a thousand miles to dump it off here," the Englishman named Hendricks said, heatedly. His wife spoke up from among the women who had dragged wooden yokes near the fire to sit on: "We would arrive in the Valley as paupers!"

"Better live paupers than dead men with property," a brother retorted, and several voices said, "Amen."

Zina's father held up his hands for quiet. "We can come back for our freight. Brother Brigham has said, 'Where the Saints do all they can, the Lord will do the rest.' I don't think the Lord intends for us to sit here and wait to be rescued."

In the end his counsel prevailed. Ellen's mother wept quietly as with the other women she sorted and discarded family treasures to lighten the load. Ellen and Joey helped her roll their clothing in a quilt and lift the pretty little cherry chest down from the wagon. From the Safford wagons, not far away, the boys were discarding the cherry rocker and Sister Eliza's step-stove. The sheet iron campstove would have to do for both families.

Soon the snow was littered with a clutter of harness, old trunks, and odds and ends of furniture. Chairs, buffalo robes, a treasured clock, heavy stoneware, brass pots, even a little organ from one of the English wagons, were discarded.

With the help of Chris and a discarded single harness, Ellen hitched her remaining ox, the one given her from the church herd, to her little wagon. It was mid-afternoon when the first wagons began to inch forward.

The oxen floundered breast-deep in snow. Short-legged, weighted down by their yokes, they had to push the snow ahead of them. It was a merciless struggle for those in the lead. Men on foot took turns wading through the snow to break a trail for the oxen.

"Hike!" Ellen shouted, goading her ox. Joey was with the men up ahead but her mother struggled along beside her. Their skirts were white from hemline to above their knees but quite dry, for the air was too chill to melt the clinging snow.

When early dusk fell they were still within sight of the abandoned freight wagons and the litter of their last camp. They had come barely a mile, at terrific effort. Ellen was numbed with cold and wearier than she could ever remember being, but her mother looked sick. Harriet's face was gray with fatigue and she had fits of shivering, like the ague.

When the welcome order came to make camp, both men and beasts were exhausted, and tempers ran short. As Ellen struggled up with her one ox, she heard a bitter voice say, "At least we're carrying our firewood with us." It was the Englishman who had been forced to leave two wagonloads of furnishings behind, and he was looking straight at Ellen's fit-out.

Chris spoke up from the men clearing a space in the snow for a fire. "The light wagon's too valuable for firewood. We should be using it to break trail."

"We don't need a Missourian to tell us what to do!" the man retorted, angrily.

An expectant hush fell over the wagon circle, as everyone looked at Chris. A Mormon boy would have swung a blow at an insult like that, but Chris stood as if frozen.

It was more than Ellen could bear. She turned from her ox's head with the harness in her hands and cried, "Burn it! Burn it! See if I care!" and burst into tears. First Buff—then Daisy—and now the little wagon—and they had not yet reached the end of the long road.

"Burn it!" she sobbed. "What does it matter, when we're going to die here, anyway, so close to the Valley?"

"Ellen!" her mother protested, helplessly, and a fit of shivering came over her.

Diantha Safford put her young arm around Harriet, saying, "Come and rest on Mama's bed, Sister Harriet. I'll fix supper." Love had gentled her young face, bringing to it an expression of sweetness reminiscent of Sister Eliza's.

Brother Safford urged his wearied horse through the snow toward them. "We'll transfer your belongings to my wagons tonight, Sister Harriet. You and Ellen can sleep with the girls in one wagon and I'll take Joey in with me and the boys." He did not seem to notice Ellen's tears.

"Yes, Brother Phineas," Harriet said, shivering, and Diantha led her away.

Chris and the other men had started a fire with wood brought in the wagons, and were piling sagebrush from the clumps they had uncovered on the flames. Ellen let her single harness lie where it dropped from her ox. She would not need it again.

She cast an oblique glance at Zina who stood outside the Safford wagons, drooping with weariness, hunched against the cold. The other girl's dark eyes met hers briefly.

"So you're through teamstering."

Ellen stiffened. "What difference does it make?"

Zina didn't answer. The difference it made lay unspoken between them. They would share a wagon tonight—maybe even huddle side by side as she and her mother and Joey had done last night to keep warm.

Sharing a bed with the person who had cut Buff's hobbles! How could they lie down together with this hate between them?

The company huddled close around the cook fires while simmering gruel and beans, soaked all day in snow water, sent clouds of fragrant vapor into the chill air. Little knots of men discussed their situation, arguing again the advisability of waiting where they were for Brother Brigham's supply wagons to reach them.

Ellen heard Brother Stewart exclaim angrily, "We cannot ask our oxen to pull us through three feet of snow! They will drop in their tracks and leave us afoot. We've *got* to wait for more stock!"

Ellen noticed that Chris was not a member of any group. He stood apart from everyone, his long face that was usually so merry closed against them all. She felt a flicker of impatience with him. Why hadn't he defended himself against their charges? He had said not a word the time she and Zina had leaped to his defense, and she had thought then it was because he was taken by surprise. But to stand silent when a man called him "Missourian" to his face!

They ate their simple meal, then gathered in a large circle for prayers. A vote was taken and it was decided to wait where they were for the supply wagons. Two men volunteered to go ahead on horses to urge haste.

A sister's thin voice rose in the first line of "Come, come, ye Saints!" and the company joined in. Brother Safford, outvoted in the matter of pushing on but still full of feeling, bore down hard on the lines:

> *"Why should we think to earn a great reward*
> *If we now shun the fight?*
> *Gird up your loins, fresh courage take. . . ."*

There were voices that quavered on the last verse:

> *"And should we die before our journey's through,*
> *Happy day! All is well!*
> *We then are free from toil and sorrow, too—*
> *All is well—all is well."*

The hymn died away on the frosty air and silently the Saints separated to climb into their wagons.

Before going to the Safford wagons, Ellen went to bid a sentimental good-by to the little wagon on which they had fastened all their hopes for getting to the Valley. In the morning it would probably feed their breakfast fire. She scuffed through the trampled snow toward it.

As she approached, a shadow moved quickly around the wagon from side to back. "Who's there?" Ellen said, sharply. But she got no answer.

For a moment she stood still, her heart pounding. Then she set her foot on the near wagon wheel spokes and, climbing lightly and quickly up, parted the wagon cover.

She looked into Chris Denham's guilty face. He was standing with his head bowed under the low cover and his arms were full of provisions.

CHAPTER 16

CHRIS!"

"Shh!" he silenced her, and stepped back so she could come in.

"Why are you stocking my wagon?" Ellen demanded, in a whisper. "What are you going to do?"

"What difference does it make? They'll chop it up for firewood if I don't take it." His face was hard and closed to her, as he set the bag of provisions down in the empty wagonbed.

"You're going to try to go on alone? Chris, you can't! You'll never make it."

"I can get your little wagon through the snow. They've been making fun of it all along, Ellen, but I've seen the way it got through the swampy bottoms and the way it made the fords. I've been trying to tell them it could break trail for the big wagons, but they won't listen to a Missourian!"

She swallowed hard. "Is that why—?"

"Sure, I'm a Missourian. I can't help it if I was born there, can I?" There was bitterness in his young voice. "They can sit here and starve and freeze, waiting to be rescued, if they want to. How do they expect the supply wagons to get through to them? The winter's just starting! Me, I'd just as soon die trying to get through."

Ellen's heart was knocking against her ribs. "You don't know the trail."

"I can get to Fort Bridger. I talked to some trappers and Injun traders back at Fort Laramie, and they told me the landmarks to look for. Long as the stars are out I can keep my team headed west. And I aim to have the best team in the company," he added, belligerently. "The old Englishman's Missouri mules!"

"He'll stop you. Somebody'll hear you."

"They're so dog-tired they won't wake," Chris said, scornfully. "They're so tired they ain't even left a guard to scare the timber wolves off what stock they got left. Tom Bedford's snoring in our wagonbed right now."

There was a hurt in her chest. It was a shameful thing that Chris, who had helped her and her mother all the long journey, had been made to feel unwanted now in the company of Saints. But the thing he was doing—taking a team and provisions and lighting out alone—was not only wrong but dangerous.

He had always been ready with comfort and advice for her when she needed it, yet she had failed to sway him from his foolhardy plan. Ellen drew a deep breath.

"All right, Chris. If you're set on going, I'll go with you."

"Like heck you will!"

"You can't do it alone! Together, we might have a chance. Don't forget I'm a teamster. I've had eight hundred miles of experience, in all kinds of weather."

"Exceptin' snow."

She was indignant. "Didn't I get through the snow this afternoon with *one ox?*"

"You've never driven mules."

"You taught me to drive an ox team," she said, tartly. "I guess you can teach me to drive mules. Please listen to me, Chris! One of us alone would likely go to sleep in this cold and never wake up. If there are two of us, we can take turns sleeping and driving. Together, we'll have a chance."

"All right," he suddenly gave in. "You better get some more foodstuffs and your buffalo robe. I'll pick up a couple of cookpots and some wood." His matter-of-factness did not hide the emotion in his voice. He wouldn't say he was glad she was going, but Ellen knew.

She trudged back through the snow to the Safford wagons, her mind busy. Something Chris said had stayed with her. The little wagon could break a trail through the snow. If she and Chris proved it could, maybe the company would take heart and follow. Or maybe they would meet the supply wagons and could bring food back to the company where the heavy freight wagons could not get through. Or perhaps they could buy supplies and fresh stock at Fort Bridger.

She knew Chris well enough to know he would turn back if it meant saving the company, in spite of the bitterness he felt toward them now. She wished she dared wake Brother Safford and get his counsel, but she knew she could not, without betraying Chris. She would have to go along with him and do the best she could.

Her mother was sleeping and Diantha had crawled into the other bed. Zina was standing with her back to the canvas flap, between Ellen and the lantern, in an attitude of waiting, but she did not turn around or speak.

The things Joey and the Safford boys had carried over from the little wagon were stacked neatly at the foot of her mother's bunk. Ellen quietly picked up the folded buffalo robes, slipping a small bag of meal and a side of bacon in between them. She had turned to go before Zina spoke.

"Where are you going?"

"To sleep in my own wagon."

"Alone?" Zina's dark eyes were wide and startled.

"Mama'll rest better. Besides—" Ellen's eyes met the other girl's straight on— "I don't relish sleeping here."

Zina bit her lip and turned her head.

I could break her down right now and make her admit she let Buff loose, Ellen thought, with a surge of anger. But she could not risk waking her mother.

She glanced at the tousled dark hair and the weath-

ered cheek that had been so smooth and high-colored
when they started the journey, and prayed that Diantha
would be gentle with her mother. But even more than
tender care, her mother needed those supplies and the
extra stock that would take their wagons safely to the
Valley.

Clutching her precious bundle in one arm, she
climbed down from the wagon, and Zina did not try to
stay her.

The fires were beds of blackened coals and the Saints
had left them for their wagons and the warmth of their
quilts. Cold stars shone in the clear sky. The snow had
hardened until it squeaked under her steps and its
surface glistened. Weather like this could freeze the
wagons in their drifts.

Her wagon was empty. When she had arranged her
buffalo robes and meager provisions, she took the trail
toward the willows where the stock had bedded down.
She met Chris returning with two big mules roped together.

"How are you going to hitch them?"

"I borried the mules—I'll borry a harness."

"We'll never get away without waking everybody."

"I've got a plan," Chris said, confidently. "I figure
most everybody'll sleep sound the first hour or so."

It was still early enough so that the noise they made
in preparation might be mistaken for a late unhitching
and feeding. Chris glanced up at the sky and whis-
pered, "Glad there's no moon."

When all was ready, he told her, "When I start 'em,

head for the willows. Don't yell at 'em, 'less you have to." He whipped the mules and boldly cried, "Hii—yiike!" Ducking, he ran low for the wagon where he and Tom Bedford had made their bed.

As Ellen urged the mules forward with her whip, she could hear him beyond the Safford wagons, still yelling, "Haw, there, bally!" What was he trying to do—wake the whole camp?

Then she heard him say, loudly, "Go back to sleep, Tom. It's only Tom Bedford, having nightmares again."

There were a few sleepy inquiries. She heard Tom's sheepish mumble. A dog barked feebly and one of her mules heehawed. Under cover of the disturbance Ellen moved farther away from the scattered wagons, down the trail already broken through the snow to the willows.

There was no jangling of pots and kegs now. The little wagon had been stripped and the only sound it made was a squeak of the axle and a crunching as the wheels packed down the snow.

When she was far enough away that the camp was obscured by some large drifts piled up against a clump of willows, she halted and waited for Chris to catch up with her. The steamy breath of the beasts made a little cloud of vapor around their bowed heads. The lone dog was barking still but his bark was faraway and widely spaced, as though his heart were not in it. Ellen stamped the creeping chill from her feet, listening for footsteps that would tell her Chris was coming.

What she heard was a sound that made her skin

prickle. It was the scratch of canvas and it came from inside the wagon. While her heart stood still, a hand parted the flap. Zina Safford's dark gypsy-like face appeared in the opening.

"You!" Ellen said.

The other girl jumped to the ground. "I didn't aim to spy! I followed because I wanted to talk to you. There's something I have to tell you, Ellen. I've been trying to say it for two days."

"I know what it is," Ellen told her, in a hard voice. "I've known it was on your conscience. You cut Buff's hobbles. It was you killed him."

"I didn't know he would die." In the starshine Ellen could see the glitter of tears in Zina's eyes. "Honest, I didn't, Ellen! I was just wanting to harass you. I don't know what makes me so hateful. Ever since the snowstorm I've been thinking how we needed every beast we had, and I've hated myself so I could hardly stand it. I wouldn't dare tell Papa what I did."

Ellen looked at her, torn between anger and pity.

"I guess I've been jealous of you from the time we left Kanesville," Zina confessed, in a shamed voice.

"You jealous of *me?*" Ellen said, in astonishment. "Land sakes, why?"

"Because you were the only girl teamster. There's nothing in the world I wanted so much as to drive a team, but with two boys in the family what chance did I have? I've envied you so, I could die!"

"I drove because I had to," Ellen said, slowly, but she could understand how Zina might have felt. There was a lot of tomboy in Zina. "I've been jealous, too." The reluctant words came out in spite of her.

"Why on earth should you?" Zina demanded, in honest surprise, and Ellen felt herself warming toward her.

"Do you remember the day you and Diantha picked out the sprigged muslin in Brother Atkins' store?" It seemed an age ago. "I wanted it so badly I could have clawed you for it."

Zina began to laugh.

Ellen stiffened. Then she felt the laughter bubbling up inside her, all warm and catchy, like tears. Zina Safford, jealous of *her!* First thing she knew, she and Zina were holding on to each other, laughing and crying together there in the lonely snow and darkness.

They did not even hear Chris until he walked around the wagon.

CHAPTER 17

THE night was long and bitterly cold. Ellen and Chris took turns driving while the other walked with Zina ahead of the mules, breaking a path. They had had no choice but to let Zina come, too.

"You've got to take me with you," she'd insisted, her face alive with mischief. "If you don't, I'll wake Brother Hendricks and tell him you're making off with his prize mules."

She was so sassy about it they couldn't help laughing. Ellen pointed out that Zina could be of help to them, and Chris had reluctantly agreed. It was Zina who said, "Papa never let us start a journey without a prayer," and led them to join hands and drop to their knees in the snow while they prayed for strength and guidance.

It was Zina, too, who kept them laughing and singing the first hours of the night. She seemed almost lighthearted now she had unburdened her conscience, and Ellen knew just how she felt. In the warm rush of forgiveness with which she had embraced Zina, all her fatigue and anxiety seemed to have fallen away.

But as the chill sank deeper and deeper into their flesh, and each step through the piled snow seemed to require more effort, all three fell silent. Chris watched the sky, keeping the North Star well to their right.

Toward midnight the mules balked and stood, shivering and obstinate, knee-deep in snow. The moon had risen, so pale and remote that it seemed to cast a blue light.

Ellen did not dare ask Chris if he thought they were still on the road. She looked back at the trail they had left. Until it snowed again, or the wind filled up their ruts, they could find their way back to the company— or the company could follow them. But if it should snow or blow— She had a frightening moment when she wondered if she would ever see her mother or Joey again.

"We'd better get some sleep," Chris said. He was hoarse with cold. "The mules won't go any farther without rest."

He took some precious sticks of wood from the wagon and, making a clearing in the snow, built a fire. When it was hot enough to dry them out, they pulled clumps of sagebrush they had uncovered, and threw them on. Once they caught, the roots burned slowly, with a hot glow.

The three of them huddled round the blaze, deliciously drowsy with the warmth, while a bucket of mash Chris had prepared for the mules heated.

"I'll keep the fire going awhile," Chris told Zina and Ellen. The two girls did not need a second invitation to climb into the wagon. Before Ellen could marvel that she and Zina were rolled up in the same buffalo robe, she had fallen into an exhausted sleep.

She wakened when the chill had seeped through the robes. She and Zina were curled together like two kittens. And she had wondered how she could sleep in the same wagon with her this night! Gently, Ellen moved away and inched out of the rolled bed so as not to waken her.

She parted the canvas flap and looked out on a gray dawning. Both moon and stars were lost in an overcast sky. Chris still slept, rolled up beside the dying fire, and the mules stood where he had fed them last night, asleep on their feet.

Ellen stirred up the fire and put on a few more pieces of wood and some sagebrush. She filled their cookpot with clean snow and set it on to melt and heat for the mush.

Chris stirred and sat up. "Snow," he muttered, looking at the sky. His yellow head swung slowly around as he studied the contours of the mountains visible now against the lightening sky. Gradually the anxious expression of his sleepy face gave way to one of wonder.

"Ellen, do you think the snow is as deep as it was back at camp?"

She looked down. "It's only about two feet here."

"It was nearly four feet deep around some of the wagons!" Chris gave an excited laugh. "See how the sagebrush pokes up through it? We were so tired last night we didn't notice. And look over there!"

She followed the line of his pointing arm and saw a large clump of willows that straggled away from them down a little valley.

"It's a spring," Chris said, impatiently. "It's the head of a creek. *And it's flowing toward the west!*"

Zina's lively face appeared in the opening in the wagontop. "What's all the excitement about?"

"Don't you see?" Chris exclaimed, jumping up and kicking aside his buffalo robes. "Before the snowstorm we were following the Sweetwater, going upstream. The road ahead follows that little creek and we'll be going *downstream*. Our company was trapped on the divide. That's why the snow was so much deeper there. Look at those mountains yonder!" He was shouting in his excitement. "They're *blue!* If we keep going, we'll run out of the snow!"

Zina jumped down from the wagon. "We'd better tell Papa," she said, and Chris looked at her in startled respect.

"Of course! If the company can make it as far today as they did yesterday, they'll be out of the deep drifts." He glanced up at the gray sky. "If they stay where they are, they'll get more snow."

Ellen's pot was boiling. She salted it and poured meal from the sack into it, a little at a time, stirring it vigorously. *They were going back!* She hoped she would never have to admit how relieved she felt.

"Papa wanted to keep traveling," Zina said, as she picked up a knife and sliced bacon for the skillet.

It was true. Ellen remembered him arguing, "I don't think the Lord intends for us to sit here and wait to be rescued." In some ways he was like her father. The thought warmed her.

"We'll leave the wagon here," Chris decided, when they had finished their breakfast.

This time Ellen did not even look back at it. They would pass this way again, but even if it should be chopped up for firewood, the little wagon had proved itself. They could follow its ruts going back and, if the snow held off a little longer, the whole company would move out on the trail it had broken. Yes, the "gypsy wagon" had served them well.

It was much faster returning, with Ellen hanging on behind Chris on the larger mule and Zina riding alone. They soon met the express riders Brother Safford had despatched to the Valley, two men on horses carrying their provisions in saddlebags. Chris gave them his news.

"Get the word to camp as soon as you can," they told him. They continued on, plainly cheered.

Before noon Ellen sighted the snowbound wagons, the bare bows of some of them like the ribs of huge skeletons half buried in drifts. From the willows below camp several horsemen came riding to meet them. They recognized Brother Safford in the lead.

His face looked gaunt and craggy as some of the rocks in the Black Hill country they had passed through. "Thank the Lord you're all safe!" he said, in stern disapproval. "You did a foolish, ill-considered thing, going off in the dark and cold to follow a road four feet under the snow. Even my express waited for daylight!"

"Papa, wait till you hear—"

"We're camped on the Continental Divide!"

"We have only to push a little farther."

Eager words poured out as all three of them at once tried to tell him that the deepest snow was under their wheels and that the road would get easier and easier.

"We were in sight of bare rocky ground, dotted with sagebrush, only a half day's travel from here," Chris finished. "The mountains have no snow except on their peaks."

Brother Safford could only shake his head from side to side. "Come, let us go and tell Sister Harriet you are safe."

In camp, an angry Englishman grabbed at the rope of their mount before Chris and Ellen could slide down. "Who gave you permission to make off with my mules?"

Brother Safford raised his hand. "Maybe the Lord moved him to take them, Brother Hendricks." Ellen saw the twinkle in his eyes. He was *very* like her father! "Chris has brought us news that could save our lives. Hitch up your oxen, and let the mules trail. The wagons are moving."

The wagons are moving! There's bare ground ahead!

The word spread quickly through camp. As Ellen and Zina walked to meet Sister Harriet, a little knot of men gathered around Chris.

"Yesterday he was the 'Missourian,' but today he's a hero," Zina observed, and Ellen laughed and squeezed her arm.

Chris had been right. She and Zina should have been friends long ago.

CHAPTER 18

THEY forded Little Sandy and Big Sandy and then crossed Big Sandy again. When the ford at the swirling Green River proved deeper than they expected, they dried out their bedding and provisions and toiled on toward Fort Bridger and the blue mountains. Each night they prayed that the full blast of winter be delayed yet a few weeks longer, and though the sky remained overcast and a cold wind blew, the storm held off.

At Fort Bridger they were able to buy a little corn for the stock and to send word of their progress ahead to the Valley by faster travelers.

"Aren't we a dragging, raggedy lot?" Zina asked Ellen, as they began to climb the high ridges. Their shoes were worn and whitened by alkali, and their clothing faded from the sun and stained with the dust they could no longer shake nor wash out.

"All but Dianthy and Tom," Ellen said, and they giggled. Those two were scarcely ever separated. Diantha filled the teamster's plate at the campfire and took her own to sit beside him. When they all knelt in prayer, Tom's arm dropped naturally over Diantha's shoulders.

"When's it gonna be?" the other teamsters never tired of asking Tom.

At last Diantha reported that she and Tom wished to be married on the Bear River, just before the wagons started down the canyon to the Valley.

"And you are to be my bridesmaids," she told Ellen and Zina. She gave Ellen a shy smile and said, "I thought maybe you could wear my sprigged muslin. It's just like Zina's, you know. I've got Mama's wedding dress."

The sprigged muslin! Ellen fingered her sun-bleached, dusty dress and felt her eyes misting.

Tired faces brightened as the plans were made. Sister Stewart and Sister Priddy—who had a high, surprisingly sweet singing voice—walked together, learning parts for the duet they would sing. Evenings after supper, the brother who had played for the dancing, brought out his fiddle and practiced wedding music.

On Saturday evening they stopped beside a stream in a beautiful narrow valley between gently rolling hills. Taking out axes and hatchets, the men felled enough willows and quaking-aspens to put up a small bower, lacing their frost-tipped branches overhead in a red-and-gold canopy.

There was a flurry of activity among the women who must bake and wash and iron for the wedding, exhausted though they were. Sister Priddy shook out a gown and asked Ellen, "There, w'ot do you think of that? It ain't seen the light of day since we left England!" She held the purple folds up against her bosom, and her dirty yellow hair looked almost golden.

The Sunday morning sun was pale and distant, but it was out for the wedding. At one side of the bower Sister Stewart and Sister Priddy stood together and sang in a blaze of color, Sister Stewart's hair a wild orange beside the purple dress.

Shivering in their sprigged muslins in spite of pretty borrowed shawls, Zina and Ellen took their places behind Diantha, who looked more than ever like an old-fashioned picture of her mother in the yellowed silk-and-lace dress.

With her hand on his arm, Hyrum Safford led his sister into the bower where their father waited, his Bible in his hand. From the other side Tom entered, with Chris beside him. Someone had loaned Chris a suit and, thin as he was, he looked a man. Ellen kept her eyes lowered and her steps even with Zina's, hearing the sprigged muslin rustle around their feet.

Everyone had grown taller this summer, in spite of the hardships, she thought. Chris. Joey. Diantha and Tom, who would soon be man and wife. Had she changed as much as they? She realized with surprise that her sixteenth birthday had come and gone unnoticed.

The fiddle had stopped and an elderly brother was praying: "—and grant that the sun shall shine on this couple who are come before Ye to take their vows; withhold Thy storms from buffeting them, as Ye withhold the winter snows from these Thy servants, that all may reach Thy promised land."

A chorus of deep and fervent "Amens." Women wiping their eyes. Brother Phineas blowing his nose and clearing his throat before beginning the marriage service.

When it was over the kissing began. Harriet came and hugged Zina and Ellen together, one in each arm. "You look so pretty, both of you—just like twins!"

"Zina, Ellen—" Ellen turned slowly toward Brother Safford. His words brought back a curious aroma—the mingled smells of calico and smoked bacon and buckskin—as she remembered the day he said, *"Diantha, Zina—you know Ellen Barlow."*

Always he had addressed his daughters together. He had given one daughter in marriage but already he was putting another in her place. "The Safford girls," people would say, and she would be one of them.

She raised her eyes to her mother's and they exchanged a long loving look. Harriet's eyes filled with tears as Ellen said, "Everything's going to be all right, Mama."

After a wedding breakfast of sidemeat and mush and hot biscuits, the women put off their finery and the men broke camp. Soon the train was moving again.

They struggled on, anxiously watching the skies and

the direction of the October wind. Over the mountains lay Zion, but between them lay the roughest part of the journey. From the summit of a ridge the country to the west looked rough and tumultuous. They descended into a canyon on a steep road with turns so sharp one wagon snapped its tongue and all behind were forced to wait while it was mended with a quaking-aspen sapling. On the canyon floor they crossed and re-crossed the creek on a road so narrow that the few canvas tops remaining were torn by the bushes. It was a relief to start climbing again.

"It's the 'long mountain!' " Brother Stewart shouted. "The last long climb!"

The word spread back through the wagons. *When we reach the summit we will see the Valley!*

Chris rode up and paced his pony to Ellen's steps. "It's nigh the end of your journey, Ellen."

"But not of yours."

"No. Not of mine." His eyes had a look of distance in them.

Brother Safford caught up with them on his big bay horse. "We'll see the Valley from the next pass," he told them, quite as if they hadn't heard. His black eyes were softer than Ellen had ever seen them. They reminded her of the soft shine of velvet. She knew he was excited, too.

"Chris," he said, "you've the makings of a fine man. We'd like to keep you with us."

"Even though I'm a Missourian?" Chris asked, wryly.

The big man's eyes twinkled. "We don't hold the

place of a man's birth against him, if he doesn't brag about it. We'll still be proud to have you."

Chris smiled at him. "Thank you, sir, but I reckon I'll push on to California where my father is."

"Maybe you'll come back some day."

Chris looked at Ellen. "I reckon I'll be coming back to the Valley."

All at once Ellen's heart was so full she thought it might burst, with a warm surge of affection that embraced everyone—not only Chris and Brother Safford, and of course her mother and Joey—but the whole ragged and worn, wonderful and funny company of Saints who had been forced to live almost like a family all summer.

As long as she could remember anything she would tell the story of the yellow-haired boy who had crossed the Missouri on the backs of the swimming oxen, of the brother who had dressed up in his wife's skirt and bonnet to milk his new cow, of the shy teamster whose nightmare stampeded the cattle but won him a pretty bride, and of the snowed-in wagon train rescued by the gypsy cart it had scorned.

They toiled up a rocky dugway and suddenly the world seemed to drop away from their feet. There were no more mountains to climb. Instead, far to the west, was a shimmer of white and ice blue.

"The lake! The salt desert!"

"It's the Valley!"

Those behind left their wagons standing on the grade and ran to the top to see the sight their eyes had hungered for. Some fell to their knees, others laughed. Some cried.

Suddenly the shouts rose again. "Look! Down in the canyon! See that cloud of dust?"

"It's a buggy!"

"Look, there are wagons behind it!"

They watched eagerly. The Safford boys climbed a rocky point to get a further view. Brother Phineas looked through his long glass, then passed it around while he wiped tears of emotion from his eyes. The dust clouds moved steadily closer until they could see the buggies and the wagons beneath them, and the men and women riding, shouting and waving white handkerchiefs. The Saints were coming to meet them, bringing wagons of provisions and extra stock and, for some, a chance to ride the last difficult miles into the Valley.

Ellen looked unbelievingly, as at a mirage. The long road to the Valley had an ending, and they had reached it. She searched the view before her for some sign that it was the end of the rainbow, as it had seemed back in those days of striving and yearning on the Missouri. But she saw only the mountains dropping away to the barren lake, and a flat benchland like desert.

Another frontier—a new life—and work to do.

"But who's afraid of work?" she asked herself, with a little smile. She knew now what she could do!

"Ellen."

She looked up at Chris, back again on the Indian pony.

"Get up behind me and ride down."

She put her foot on his in the stirrup and gave him her hand. He pulled her up behind him, a-straddle the horse. She tucked her full skirt firmly around her legs and grasped his waist.

Chris touched the flank of his pony and they began the descent into the Valley.

EPILOGUE

ALMOST before they could unpack their wagons and move into their new log houses, the Mormons found their refuge invaded by gold-seekers on the way to California. But the pioneers resisted the lure of the gold fields and remained in Utah Territory, industriously planting crops and selling their produce to the travelers to California.

Summer after summer, new and old friends crossed the plains by wagon train to join the Saints, many coming from England and the Scandinavian and other European countries. Some even walked across the plains, pushing their belongings in hand carts. The city they built where the bench of the Wasatch Mountains reaches down to the shores of the Great Salt Lake became known as Salt Lake City, and their other communities spread out into what is now Idaho, Wyoming and Nevada.

Their enemies did not forget them and in 1876, a United States "army" was sent out from Washington to subdue them. But it was a bloodless war and twenty years later, their long differences finally resolved, Utah was admitted to the Union, with Salt Lake City—even more beautiful than Nauvoo—as its state capital.